## ALSO BY HELEN FROST

*Keesha's House*
*Room 214: A Year in Poems*
*The Braid*
*Diamond Willow*
*Crossing Stones*
*Salt*

# HELEN
# FROST

**SQUARE
FISH**
FRANCES FOSTER BOOKS
FARRAR STRAUS GIROUX
NEW YORK

An Imprint of Macmillan
175 Fifth Avenue
New York, NY 10010
mackids.com

Square Fish books may be purchased for business or promotional use. For information on
bulk purchases, please contact the Macmillan Corporate and Premium Sales Department
at (800) 221-7945 x5442 or by e-mail at specialmarkets@macmillan.com.

Library of Congress Cataloging-in-Publication Data
Frost, Helen, date.
Hidden / Helen Frost.
p. cm.
Summary: When fourteen-year-olds Wren and Darra meet at a Michigan
summer camp, both are overwhelmed by memories from six years earlier when
Darra's father stole a car, unaware that Wren was hiding in the back.
ISBN 978-1-250-05684-9 (paperback)
[1. Novels in verse. 2. Interpersonal relations—Fiction. 3. Camps—Fiction.
4. Memory—Fiction. 5. Blame—Fiction. 6. Michigan—Fiction.] I. Title.
PZ7.5.F76You 2011     [Fic]—dc22          2010024854

Originally published in the United States by Farrar Straus Giroux
First Square Fish Edition: 2015
Book designed by Jay Colvin
Square Fish logo designed by Filomena Tuosto

1  3  5  7  9  10  8  6  4  2

AR: 3.9 / LEXILE: HL670L

*Dedicated with love*
*to Chad*
*who swims me safely home*
*every time*

# CONTENTS

# PART ONE

## *The Way You Might Remember Your Best Friend*

*Wren Abbott*

*1*

I was a happy little girl wearing a pink dress,
   sitting in our gold minivan,
     dancing with my doll, Kamara.

      *I'll be right back,* Mom promised.
      *Leave the music on,* I begged,
        so she left her keys
        dangling
     while she
        ran in to pay for gas
        and buy a Diet Coke.

*2*

I think about that little girl
    the way you might remember your best friend
        who moved away.
      Sitting in the middle seat
        beside an open window,
        her seatbelt fastened,
         she looked out at the world.

**3**

And then she heard
    a gunshot
    from inside the store.

That's when she—when I—
    stopped breathing.
        I clicked my seatbelt off,
        dived into the back, and
        ducked down on the floor
            to hide
                under a blanket
                until Mom
                came back out.

I heard the car door open, heard it close.
    The music stopped.
    Why? Mom liked that song.

I breathed again. (Mom smelled like cigarettes.)

I pushed the blanket off my face,
    opened my mouth
    to ask,
        *What happened in there?*

But then I heard a word Mom wouldn't say.
    A man's voice.
    *C'mon! Start!* He was yelling at our car—
        and the car
        obeyed him.

It started up
just like it thought
Mom was driving.


*4*
Who *was* driving?
Had this man just shot someone? Had he
shot . . . Mom?
If he found out I was back there
what would he do to me?
I pulled the blanket back over my face.
(Pretend you're Kamara.
Don't breathe. Don't move.
Be as small as you can—smaller.)


Sand on the floor of the car. I pressed hard.
It stuck to my skin.
I pressed harder.
(Breathe
if you have to,
but don't move a muscle.)


Like a small rabbit
that knows a cat is close by,
I paid attention. I didn't
twitch.


*5*
I could tell which way we were headed—
we stopped at the King Street stoplight.
Left turn . . . right turn . . . left . . .

He sped up.
Was he trying to throw the police off our trail?

He stopped, got out of the car.
Where were we?
He got back in,
                drove off faster.

Sirens?
    Yes—coming closer!

One time in first grade,
    a police officer came to our class.
        "If someone tries to grab you," she said,
        "wave your arms, kick your legs.
        Yell at the top of your lungs,
        THIS MAN IS NOT MY FATHER."

The sirens meant
    someone might stop us—
        I could jump up.
        I could wave.
        I could yell.

But it didn't happen.
We drove faster, farther.
    The sirens
        faded away in the distance.

Long straight road . . . curvy road . . .

Fast for a while. No stops.
    Right turn.
    Left turn.
        Stop. Go. Turn . . .
        I swallowed the panic that rose.
            I didn't throw up.

*6*

Sound of gravel. Dust in my throat.
(Don't cough!)
Bumping along that dusty road,
    screaming inside.
    (Dad, where are you? Mom?)
        A phone rang—Dad's ring on Mom's phone!
        Mom must have left her phone in the car.
            Her whole purse, down on the floor?

    (Do not—do not!—jump up and grab it.)
    I clenched my hands together.

*GPS,* the man snarled—I heard him dump
        Mom's purse upside down.
        He opened a window.
        He closed it.

(Did he just toss Mom's phone out the window?)

7

I put my thumb in my mouth
    like a little baby. I pulled my knees
        to my chin, and closed my eyes tight.


Where were we going?
What would happen to me when we got there?


After a long time—
    it felt like hours—
        the car slowed down.
    We made a sharp turn.
We stopped.
He got out.
I heard a garage door open.
He got back in the car.
    Forward.
    Stop.
    The garage door came down.
        The car door opened, slammed shut.
    I heard a dog.
        Barking or growling?
        In the garage or outside?
Another door opened
        and closed.
        Had the man gone somewhere?


8

Carefully, I pushed back the blanket
    and looked around.

I was alone
in a very dark place.

I might have been wrong about Mom's phone.
I kept my head low,
climbed into the middle seat,
leaned far enough forward
so I could see into the front.
Mom's water bottle—not quite empty.
A chocolate chip granola bar.
Kleenex.
ChapStick.
Checkbook.
Calendar.
Her little album of pictures—
me and Alex, her and Dad.


No wallet—she took that into the store.
No phone.


*9*
Where was I?
A messy garage—rakes and shovels,
gas cans and broken-down boxes.

In the garage door,
higher than I could reach,
three small windows,
a few rays of sun shining through them.

Behind an old freezer—
a door—to outside?

A red-and-white boat
on a trailer
right next to the car.

If I could get out fast enough, he'd never know I was there.
    I told myself what to do, and I did it:
        Quietly—get out of the car with Kamara.
        Take the granola bar. Leave the water—
            if I take that, he might notice it's gone.
        Carefully tiptoe across the floor.
            (The dog—outside—still growl-barking.)
        Squeeze behind the freezer.
            Try to open the side door.

        Locked
            with a padlock
            the size of my fist.

*10*

The freezer was empty, unplugged—it wouldn't be cold.
Could I get inside, and hide there?
    No. A boy on the news
        got stuck inside an old freezer—
    he suffocated to death
        before his mom found him.
            I shivered.

The boat?
    I might be tall enough
        to climb in
        if I stepped up on the trailer.

But I didn't dare move.

## 11

I don't know how long
    I stood there
    in my pink dress,
    mostly hidden
    behind the freezer.

## 12

A light came on. A door opened.
    I stopped breathing.

From another room, I heard
    happy voices—
        real people or on a TV?
        It was a TV—this was someone's house.

The man came out,
    opened the car door, closed it,
    went back inside.
    I was pretty sure
        he didn't look
            over at me.

## 13

I had to do something.
I ran to the boat
    and climbed in.
It was full of fishing stuff:
    nets and ropes
    a tackle box
    fishing poles
    a rusty coffee can.

    A blue cloth, partly stretched
        over the boat—
        could I hide under that?

At the boat's pointed end, a triangular place,
    like a little cave—I just fit.

A gray rag?
No—an old sweatshirt
    wadded up on the floor of the boat.
    I put it on—it covered my dress.
Yes,
    I could hide in the boat
    for a while.

## 14

I was hungry. Mom always said,
    *Eat something, Wren. It helps you think.*
        I unwrapped the granola bar, took one bite.
        One more. Another.
I tried to think.

Could I open the garage door?
If it was something to lift—could I lift it?
What if you had to know certain numbers to push?

If the door opened, he'd hear me.

Sooner or later, he'd leave the house. He had to.
Did anyone live there with him?

The dog barked louder.
It was outside, but not far away.
Had anyone fed it?

Through the windows in the garage door,
the sky
got darker and darker.

15
Someone turned on a light
and opened the door from the house.

*I thought I heard something out here.*
(A girl's voice?)

I didn't move, curled up in the boat,
clutching Kamara so hard
I thought she might break.

The man again, from inside:
*Shut that door! Stay out of there!*
*You heard me—I SAID—*

The light went off. The door slammed shut.
It sounded like somebody banged up against it.
  The girl yelled, *Ow! Quit it! That hurt!*
Then it got quiet.
After that,
 for a long time,
 nothing happened.


*16*
The garage door went up.
The light came on.
 Somewhere outside, a car door opened and closed.
I heard someone
 walk through the garage
 and open the door to the house.


A woman's voice: *What's this car doing here?*
The man: *How many times do I have to tell you—*
  *stay out of my business.*
The woman: *You keep a stolen car in our garage,*
  *it's my business.*


The light went off.
The garage door closed.
The other door slammed.
I heard shouting inside the house.
I couldn't hear words,
 but the man's voice was loud
  and mean.

## 17

I was shaking.
    Trying hard not to cry.
How could I sleep
    in the crowded boat?
I was thirsty.
Hungry.
I had to pee.

## 18

The light came on. The door from the house flew open.
    The woman: *This is the car they're searching for!*
        *What happened*
        *to Wren Abbott?*

    A voice on TV: *Once again,*
        *the child is eight years old.*
        *Last seen wearing a pink dress,*
        *with matching beads in her hair.*
        *She may be holding a doll*
        *she calls Kamara.*
        *If you have any information*
        *please call—*

## 19

The TV cut off.
The man: *Nothing to do with me!*
    *You think I'm some kind of pervert,*
    *taking a little kid?*

(What's a pervert?)

The woman: *Of course not. But, West,*
    *did you check the backseat*
    *when you got in the car?*

(The man's name is West.)

West: *No! There wasn't time!*
    *None of this worked like we planned, Stacey.*
    *No one was going to get shot.*

(*Who* got shot?)
(The woman is Stacey.)

I heard the car doors—opening, closing.

Stacey: *She's not in the car.*
    *Where is she?*

West: *Maybe she got out when I stopped*
    *in the parking lot—I took a few minutes*
    *to take the plate off another car*
    *and put it on this one.*

(That time he stopped—could I have jumped out?)

Stacey: *If she was lost in a parking lot,*
    *someone would have found her by now.*
    *They've been searching for more than six hours!*

West: *They can keep searching.*
*Tomorrow, we paint the car.*
*We ditch it.*
*Nothing to pin on me.*

Stacey: *West—this girl is Darra's age!*
*We can call from a pay phone—anonymously—*
*tell them Wren Abbott is not in the car they're searching for.*
*At least we know that much!*

(The girl is Darra.)

West: *We know NOTHING. You hear me?*
Stacey: *Let go of me!*

I'd never heard
the sound of one person hitting another,
but I knew
that was what happened.

Stacey stopped talking.
Started crying.

The door slammed again.
More yelling. Crashing sounds.
Silence.

**20**
The door opened.
Darra's voice:
*Stay out here tonight.*

*He won't hurt you if you stay out of his way.*
*I bet you're hungry. Here's some food and water.*

The door closed.

> (Who was she talking to?
> Does she know I'm here?)

Someone (Darra?) was in the garage.
   Moving around . . .
   coming closer . . .
      Right in the boat with me!
      I yelped! I couldn't help it.
   *Yeeoooww.*
A cat!
   Scratching my face. Barely missing my eye.
      We looked at each other.

   Carefully, I reached out to pet it.
      After a while, we both calmed down.
         It curled up in my arms and purred.

**21**
When the cat
jumped out of the boat,
I watched it.
   A litter box?
   Not too far away.
Maybe I could . . .
   I had to.
   I did.

I got back in the boat. The cat came too.
 It settled beside me.


 We fell asleep.


22
When I woke up, the cat was gone.
A few rays of light
 came in through the windows.
I watched the light move
 from one window
 to another.


23
I smelled cigarettes.
 West was in the garage.


I heard the door open.
Darra: *Daddy, I'm hungry.*
West: *Tell your mother.*
Darra: *Mommy has a headache.*
West: *Tell her I said to quit crying and get up and feed you.*
 *And tell her I need her out here.*


I was hungry too.
 My stomach was growling.
(Stomach, please, please be quiet. He'll hear you.)


24
I smelled
 the kind of ointment

you put on something that hurts.
    (Stacey?)

Darra: *Archie, where are you?*
    (The cat?)
    *Here, Archie!*
    (Yes. They call the cat Archie.)

Darra might look in the boat for her cat.
    Should I try to look like a gray sweatshirt
    wadded up on the floor of the boat
    under the blue boat-cover?
        Or
    should I let Darra see me?

    I didn't know who I could trust.
        I stayed quiet.
        I hid.

25
West: *Hand me a can of spray paint.*
    *No, not that one! Dark green!*
    (He never thanks her
        when she does what he says.)
Stacey: *We should open the door*
    *and get some fresh air in here.*
West: *I'm not taking chances. Someone*
    *could drive by and see what we're doing.*

It hurt to breathe.
My eyes watered.
My throat burned.


Stacey: *Darra, you better go back inside.*
      *I don't want you breathing these fumes.*
I heard Darra go in and come right back out.


Darra: *Mommy, those people are on TV again.*
Stacey: *Turn it up.*
West: *Turn it off.*
The TV got louder.
      (Darra is brave.)
News voice: . . . *Wren Abbott, age eight,*
      *missing since yesterday.*


West: *I said TURN IT OFF!*
I heard my dad's voice!
      . . . *keep the car.*
      *Just return our daughter to us.*
          *Wren, if you hear this, try*
          *to get to a phone and call home.*


He said "us."
      Dad and Alex?
      Or could it mean
          Mom was alive?
A knot inside me loosened a little.


West: *DARRA! I SAID TURN IT OFF!*
      The TV voices stopped.

*AND SHUT THAT DOOR!*
The door closed.

(*How* could I get to a phone?)

**26**
West: *Good enough.*
> *By the time the paint dries,*
> *it will be dark out.*
> *I'll drive the pickup. You two will*
> *follow in this car. We'll leave it*
> *in the mall parking lot.*

> *No one will ever know*
> > *it's been here.*

They all went inside. I let myself cough, just a little.

(Will anyone ever know *I've* been here?)

**27**
The door opened again.
> Who was in the garage?
Stacey: *Darra, if you wanted to hide out here,*
> > *where would you hide?*
Darra: *In there, I guess.*
Stacey: *What? No! Don't you ever*
> > *get inside an old freezer!*
> *I keep meaning to take the door off it.*
> *Oh . . . thank God, she's not . . .*

Darra: *Whenever Archie gets scared of Dad,*
   *he goes in the boat.*

I could jump out and pretend
   it was some kind of game.
      Hide and seek: *Found me!*
      But would Darra and Stacey hide me?

West might come out any minute.

*28*
I felt someone touch my knee.
I didn't move. I squeezed my eyes shut.

Darra: *No, Mom, she's not in the boat.*
Stacey: *Where could she be?*

They went back inside.

*29*
Darra came out again.
*Here you go. Here's some more food.*
   *I cleaned the litter box.*
   I knew she was talking to Archie.
   But maybe to me too?
The door closed.

*30*
Could I get in our car
   and hide in the backseat?

Stacey would drive to the mall,  .
    leave the car.
        I'd get out
        and find someone to help me.
Except—
    what if West changed his mind
    and drove our car?
Or—if Stacey saw me,
    what would she do?
    She was scared of him too.


    If Darra sat in the back, and found me,
    would she tell her mom I was there?
    Would they tell West?


I didn't dare try it.


## 31
What if
    I hid under the boat,
        near the garage door,
        and slipped out when the door opened,
        quickly, before it went down?
        It was dark outside.
    I could hide until both cars were gone,
        and then—start walking?


Not much of a plan, I knew,
    but it was all I had.

**32**

I climbed out of the boat, holding Kamara,
    got down on the floor and hid
        under the boat,
          right next to the garage door.


**33**

They came out.
Stacey: *West, you'd better drive this car.*
    *I can't see out of my left eye.*
    *I'll drive the truck.*
West: *You can see fine. You've driven*
    *with swollen-up eyes before.*
Stacey: *I don't want Darra in the car if it's stopped.*
West: *No one's looking for a woman and kid.*
    *Stop wasting my time. Let's get this done.*

West went back inside.
    He must have gone out another door
        to his truck.

Stacey: *Come on, Darra.*
Darra: *Should I put all the stuff back in this purse?*

I almost jumped up:
    *Don't touch my mom's stuff!*
    But I was too scared
        to make a sound,
        too scared to move.
    And I had a plan.
    It was almost time.

34

The garage door went up.
Stacey backed out in our car—dark green now.
    Gravel crunched
    as she drove away,
        and my last piece of Mom
           disappeared.


        West backed a red pickup
        around a curve in the driveway.


    The garage door started down.


I rolled underneath it.
    No houses in sight, no lights.

35

A huge white dog
    lunged at me.


    Growling.

36

It happened so fast—
    the door almost down.


The dog right there by my face.


    I rolled back under the door,
        to the only safe place I had.

I was alone
  on the hard cement floor
  beside the closed door.

Where was my shoe?
The dog stopped barking.
(Why?)

37
I thought:
I could go in the house while they're gone.
  There might be a phone in there.
    Once I was inside,
    I'd find another way out.

*What do you think, Kamara?* I asked.

Kamara said: *Try.*

I reached for the doorknob.
It turned!
  I pushed—
    the door was chained shut
    from the other side.

Through the crack I could see
  a telephone on a table.
  A box of crackers.
  A half-full glass of orange juice.

All out of reach.
I pulled the door shut.


38
I was so hungry!
    It was a whole day since
        I'd emptied the last few crumbs
        from the granola bar wrapper.


Archie's dish . . .
        Cat food?
        The dry kind.


(Pretend it's Grape-Nuts
    without any milk.)
        I ate a handful,
        left half for Archie.
    And then
        I climbed back into the boat.


39
I'd never get out.
    I couldn't stop crying.
    I wiped my nose on the sleeve of the sweatshirt.
    Smell of cigarettes. Sweat. Dead fish?
        West.
    I cried harder.


40
*Archie?*
He leapt into the boat

and dropped a dead mouse in my lap.
I tried not to scream, even though
there was no one to hear me.

(Who let him in? When?
Are there mice in here?)

Paws on my face,
soft—no claws.
Archie licked my tears,
lay down beside me,
and purred.
*I know you're here,* he was saying.

41
Archie jumped out of the boat
and stood by the door to the house.
He looked back once—
checking
to make sure
I was watching.
And then I saw,
almost hidden
inside a box turned on its side
on the garage floor
a few feet away from the door—
was it a sandwich . . .
in a plastic bag?
Beside a bottle of water?

## 42

It must have been Darra
　　who put it there.
　　(For me?)
If I was fast,
　　I could climb out and get it.
　　One leg out of the boat—
　　　　I heard wheels crunching on gravel.
　　　　The garage door started to open.
　　　　I dived back in
　　　　　　and hid.


## 43

They argued
　　as they walked
　　from the truck to the house.

Stacey: *We have to!*
West: *We don't. And we won't.*

When they got inside,
　　Stacey's voice got louder,
　　then softer,
　　until it was so quiet
　　I couldn't understand any words.

West, shouting: *You'll get the phone back*
　　*when I'm good and ready*
　　*to give it to you.*
　　*Forget you ever heard of this girl.*

*It's nothing*
*to do with us.*

Was Stacey crying?

**44**

I stayed quiet for a long time. Then
I crept out to get the sandwich and water.
    I took them back in the boat,
    ate and drank.
    I closed my eyes and pretended
        I was in the big green chair at home
            with Alex
            when we were little enough
            to fit in Dad's lap.
    I told Kamara
        all Dad's old stories.
    I tried to remember our songs.

*Michael, row the boat ashore, hallelujah* . . .
    I thought of Dad singing
    and rocking us
        like he was rowing a boat.
    Mom in the doorway,
        watching and humming along,
        then the two of them singing together,
        *The River Jordan is deep and wide,*
        *milk and honey on the other side.*
    Could I float on their voices
        into sleep
        and wake up in my own warm bed?

45

I rocked myself.

    *Archie?* I whispered. *Where are you? Come back.*

    But he didn't.


46

I fell asleep.


47

When I woke up,

    the moon shone through a window.

Someone was drumming—

        strong, like a clear, steady heartbeat.

Was I dreaming?

    I heard singing.

        Not Mom and Dad. Not

        my own voice, humming a song for Kamara.

    Like a choir

        singing to me.

        Different languages, all the same song.

Outside the boat—

    soft footsteps came closer and closer,

    stepping in time to the music.

(Who's out there?)

I leaned over the edge of the boat.
  *Here, Archie,* I whispered.

But it wasn't Archie, the orange-striped cat.

Black shiny fur, bright eyes,
    white stripes:
        a skunk was staring at me.

48
How could a skunk get in the garage?

    It turned from me, walked away, looked back.
        (Yes, I'm right here. I'm watching.)

I got out of the boat with Kamara,
and followed—
around a pile of boxes.
    (Don't knock them over, don't make a sound!)
Close to the floor, in a corner,
    the skunk's tail, black and white,
        swished through a small door.

Archie's door?
    (Could I fit through? What if I get stuck halfway?)
        (Where is the dog? Is it chained?)

Archie came in through the little door, looked at me,
    went back out, came back in,

rubbing his head on my ankles,
nudging me: *Yes, you can do it.*


## 49

I put my head through—
    the sky was dark, but the moon was bright.


One shoulder. Two shoulders. Both arms out.
    The big white dog was asleep in the dirt
        beside a gray doghouse.
        (How long is that chain?)


    The skunk was waddling toward it.


I twisted my body,
pulled my legs through.
    I was out in the moonlight.


The dog stood up,
        stretched.
            Saw me.
            Growled.


I froze.


The skunk lifted its tail. The dog yelped,
    and I ran—past the skunk, past the dog,
    down the long driveway, in one shoe
    and the big gray sweatshirt.

Clutching Kamara like life itself.
Leaving Archie
    and Darra
        behind.

# Part Two

## *It's All Her Fault*

*Darra Monson*

## I Had This Plan

I woke up from a very weird dream: A cartoon skunk sprayed Dad
and danced in our yard. Then I smelled a skunk
for real. I wanted to find out if Wren Abbott
had found the sandwich I left for her on the garage floor. I used
the kind of plastic bag that zips up tight, so no ants
would get in. I can't believe I thought of that.
I was eight years old, and I was sure I'd figured out a way to
get Wren out of our garage without anyone
finding out she'd been there—not even Mom
(and especially not Dad). I couldn't let Wren see me. I'd have
to get her out before Dad woke up, which was
usually at seven-thirty. My clock said 5:14 a.m.
I wrote a note: "Put this on." I drew a picture of a girl wearing a
blindfold, and clipped it to a scarf. I went out to the
garage. The sandwich was gone! I put the blindfold
in the same place the sandwich had been. I went inside. My next job
was to make sure she'd wear it. *Do exactly*
*what I say*, I planned to whisper through the door.
Once she put it on, I'd lead her out. Then the hard part: making
sure she didn't take the blindfold off until I led her
away, and then got myself out of sight. I'd have to

threaten her a little—maybe a lot—and there might be some parts
of the plan that could go wrong, but I hoped
I could get her to the crossroads and make her
promise not to watch which way I went. If she was scared enough of
Dad, maybe she'd do what I said. I knew
there might be people driving by—everyone
would be on the lookout for her. I'd make her hide if I saw any cars.
(We'd lie down in the ditch beside the road.)
I still wonder if it would have worked.

*Wren Abbott's Fault*

Something went wrong. I've always wished Archie could talk—he
would have told me how Wren got out.
I never told anyone my plan.
If I had pulled it off, Dad would never have known how I saved
him from getting caught. Why tell him—or Mom—
what didn't happen? When Wren didn't come to get
the blindfold, I went out in the garage to look. She wasn't curled up
in the boat. Not in the freezer. Not
hiding under the boat. She wasn't there.
I found stuff under the tarp—a granola bar wrapper, a pink shoe for
a doll (they said on the news she had a doll,
dressed like her), a dead mouse, the plastic
bag from the sandwich. So I was right—she'd been there. But four
hours later, I was sitting in a gray room
at Child Protective Services, waiting for Mom
to come and get me. Dad was looking at who-knew-how-many years
in prison. I didn't know that yet, but I was thinking:
*This is all Wren Abbott's fault. She might be cute*
*in her little pink dress, with her matching doll. But if it wasn't for*
*her, none of this would be happening.*
The last thing Dad told me before

they "detained him for questioning" (what the reporter said on the
news that night), was, *Darra,*
*can you do something for me?*
I said yes before I found out what it was. *Don't let her sell my boat.*
Why would Mom sell the boat? Weren't we all going
up to the lake for a whole week that next summer?

## Whoosh!

What do you do when all of a sudden your dad is gone and the
rest of your life is nothing
like it was before? We had *plans*
to go back to the lake—we'd be going back every summer!
Dad and Mom had already saved up almost
all the vacation and money they needed.
And then, *whoosh!* First Dad lost his job, and "started a business"—I
pictured him fixing cars for people,
with his business partner, named Stu.
*(Like beef stew?* I thought when I heard that.) But it turns out Stu was
already on a Most Wanted list
before he even met my dad, and they
weren't fixing cars, they were stealing them. They stole seven
cars—I remember every one of them. They'd
bring them into our garage and paint them.
Mom and Dad started fighting a lot. Mom hated Stu. She said Dad
should stay home and take care of me while she
went to work. Dad was okay most of the time—I
thought it would be fun, and it was, at first. Then one time he took
me with him to "pick up a car at Stu's place,"
and I caught on. It didn't take long to figure out

that Mom knew what Dad was doing, and neither of them wanted me
to tell. I never said a word about it. When I saw
the first part of the TV news about Wren Abbott,
I wondered: Did the store-robber who took the car ever go out fishing
with his kid? I knew it couldn't be Dad because he
would never rob a store. Then they showed a picture
of a man who got shot by the store clerk. It was Stu, right there on
our TV. He was dead. I thought fast. Maybe
no one besides Mom and me knew that Dad was
Stu's partner—which meant Dad might not get caught. There was a
chance. If Wren Abbott hadn't led the cops
to our house that morning, Dad would probably
still be home with us. My family would have gone back to the lake
that summer, and all five summers since.
We might be heading up there right now.

*Even the Ripples Were Gone*


There was going to be a trial, but Dad decided to plead guilty when
he saw the evidence against him. The detectives
found Bilbo chewing on a girl's shoe that morning
when they stopped at our house. How did he get the shoe? We
didn't see it when we fed him. I tried to tell them
it was mine, but (like Cinderella's ugly sisters)
when they asked for the matching one, I didn't have it. They were
all over that in a minute. *I have to inform you*
*that it matches a shoe Wren Abbott*
*had on at the time she was found.* I already knew she'd turned up at
an Amish farmhouse early that morning,
wearing Dad's sweatshirt, missing one shoe.
That much was on the news, but as soon as anyone started asking the
interesting questions (*Where were you? How*
*did you get out? Did you have anything to eat?*),
Wren wouldn't say a word. It was like when you toss stones in a lake,
the way those questions disappeared from the news;
in a couple of days, even the ripples were gone.
Who cared about Dad (or me and Mom)? It seemed like, once Dad
got locked up—end of story. I've hated Bilbo
ever since. What kind of dog betrays its own family?

Before it happened, Dad yelled at us a lot, and hit us. So I didn't
think I'd miss him much. But one day, after he was
gone, I picked up one of his old shirts and held it
to my face so I could breathe in that Dad-smell. *What?* I started to yell
at Mom. *This smells like laundry soap!*
*Who said you could wash it?* I pitched
a total fit, like I was two years old. Mom just stood there looking at
me, waiting for me to finish, not mad, but not
sympathetic either. Then she said, *Darra—*
*guess what? Dad's going to be gone a while. It's just the two of us,*
*and it won't be easy. If you want to get mad*
*at someone, and I'm the only one around—*
*go ahead. It won't hurt me. But think about it. Is this what we want?* So
I calmed down, and after that,
I tried to treat Mom better. Sometimes
we fought a little, but mostly we got along. There wasn't much
I could control about my life and that was
one thing I could do to make things better.

## Visiting Room

For six years, I've tried to figure out what happened. Dad swears he
didn't know Wren was in the garage, and Mom
claims she didn't either. Which one of them has
lied to me for almost half my life? Someone had to let her out. I didn't
think it was Mom, and I couldn't get Dad to admit
it was him—so I stopped asking. I only had
an hour twice a month, if that, to visit Dad. I decided I'd rather know
how he was doing than pester him
with questions he didn't want to answer.
I tried to act like this cheerful little kid who loved her dad. I
never told him any of my problems, or
gave him any information about Mom I knew
he wouldn't like. I kept that up for four years. The room where I saw
Dad all those Saturday afternoons was cold and gray,
so I'd wear yellow and purple and orange and green.
I'd go in with my plastic bag full of dimes and quarters, and buy him
Doritos and Coke from the vending machines.
The other people—visitors and prisoners—
all knew whose kid I was. I'd see them talking, laughing, crying—
I'd try not to listen. Those were
the only hours any of us had together.

It was private. When Mom told Dad she wanted a divorce, the
last time we went to see him, I didn't know
she wouldn't be taking me there anymore.
(She thought it wasn't good for me.) Dad knew, though. That day,
he hugged me longer than he usually did.
*What should I do about the boat if we move*
*out of the house?* I asked. He gave me the number of someone he
had met in prison who'd been released.
*He'll keep it for me until I get out,* Dad said.
I walked out through three steel doors and heard them lock. I got
back in the car with Mom, and we drove away.
A few months later, the divorce came through—
a pile of papers in the mail. Mom said, *I'm sorry, Darra,* as she laid
them on the counter. Then she got a new job, in
another town. We moved. Dad's friend came to get
the boat, and I thought about two things as I watched him drive it off:
Fishing at sunrise with Dad when I was seven.
And how Bilbo helped Wren Abbott steal my dad.

# PART THREE

## *The Diving Raft*

*Wren Abbott and Darra Monson*
Camp Oakwood
Upper Peninsula, Michigan

## Here I Am
### Wren


I thought this day would never come,
but here I am, sitting on the top bunk
    on the window side
    of Girls Cabin Eight,
    the best bed
    in the best cabin
    at Camp Oakwood,
    the best camp
    in the world.

I always try to get here first so I can pick the bed I want—
    one where I can wake up early,
        look out at the lake,
            and watch the sun come up
            behind the flagpole.
    I love Lake Josephine,
        and I like knowing
            the Great Lakes are close by.

I can see the check-in table.
    There's Savannah—her sister Zoe

must be in Cabin One. It's her first time at camp.
Savannah's been scrunched up in the backseat
    between Zoe and a footlocker
    for two hours.
I'll go help her carry in her stuff, which she always has a ton of.

She sees me coming.
    *Wren!* she screams. We hug.
Toryn runs over to the check-in table.
We all talk at once.
*We're in Cabin Eight! K.C.'s our counselor again!*
*Wait till you see Rachel.*

*There's Chen and Meghan,* says Toryn,
    *and Meghan's little brother, Sam.*
They're in the parking lot,
    taking their suitcases from the back of the camp van,
        just in from the airport run.
Last year, Chen brought
    a different color outfit for each day—
    it looks like she's still wearing blue on Saturdays.

Just the opposite of Rachel, who always brings
    two pairs of shorts,
    eight black T-shirts,
    hiking boots, and
    a Padres cap. Here she comes.
    Dressed in black like always,
        but whoa!
Toryn states the obvious:
    *Your hair is orange!*

*I know,* says Rachel. *Yours is boring brown.*

I check to see if Toryn is offended.
    No. I didn't think she would be.
    We can dress and look
        however we want—
           at camp, nobody cares—
           we're all good friends.

And this year, for the first time,
I get to stay
for all six weeks!

## "For Darra, Four Weeks"
### Darra

I'm looking at my list of what they told us to bring: good shoes, a
warm jacket ("The summer nights
can get chilly!"), a flashlight ("for those
middle-of-the-night trips to the bathroom"). So cheerful. "Girl
products" listed along with shampoo and
toothpaste—that's subtle. No cell phones.
Does anyone here even know it costs money to keep a cell phone on?
No alcohol or drugs—why is this check-in
lady looking at me like she's not sure if
she should go through my bags? *You'll get used to not having TV,*
she brightly tells me. *Your cabin is right up that*
*path. Do you think you can find it?* Yes—I can
read a map. Girls Cabin Six. Girls Cabin Seven. Girls Cabin Eight.
How original—let's put the cabins in a
straight line and number them. Duh.
Plus it looks like nothing has changed here in the past forty years,
so I've seen it all in Grandma's pictures. She'd
talk about this camp "up in the U.P." (which means
Upper Peninsula, but I used to think it was "You Pee"), as if her old
friends were still teenagers here and she wished
I could step in where she left off. Then she dies,

and her will says, "For Darra, four weeks at Camp Oakwood." Like,
just because she puts that in writing, I'm
supposed to be thrilled to come here,
where I don't know anyone, and all these rich girls stare at me
when I get out of our crappy car, as if
I dropped in from some other planet.
Mom and I had to leave at six-fifteen this morning. What was
I thinking, to convince myself the seven-
hour drive to get here might be worth it?
Now everyone's standing around in these little clumps. I'm alone.
When the check-in lady asks me if I can find
Girls Cabin Eight, one of the clumps half turns,
like they're all one person, and looks me over. I'm positive they're in
my cabin, but not one of them says hello.
They watch me as I walk past them, past
the dining hall, up the path to the cabin. *Darra? I'm K.C. There's a*
*bed right here for you, if you want to*
*put your things down,* the counselor chirps.
The bed beside hers? Um—no thanks, I'll just get back in the car
and go home now. Mom is still at the office,
paying for this. There's time. *Or—that one.*
A bottom bunk in the middle, between two other bunks—with some
kind of stain on the mattress. Whatever.
A boy comes to the door. *Josh is in our cabin.*
*Can we borrow your ramp?* he asks. K.C. nods. *Go ahead.* The guy—
his name is Jeremy—sizes me up. *Give me*
*a hand here?* he asks. I shrug. *Each cabin*
*is supposed to have its own ramp. It looks like someone stole*
*ours,* he says. *You take that end.*
Like he thinks I'm planning to stay.

## Wait a Minute
### Wren


Rachel wants to see the new kiln in the pottery barn,
    but Savannah has to find out
        what boys are back,
        so we take the long way,
        past their cabins.
*Wait—look—* Savannah says, *there's that new girl,*
        *helping Jeremy. You couldn't pay me*
        *to drag a heavy ramp through the dirt like that.*

We walk over to them, and Meghan asks Jeremy
    what he's doing. *It's for Josh,* he says.
*They made a walkway down to the lake*
        *so he can swim with us.*
        *He might even learn to sail.*
        *He's around here somewhere, showing Derek his*
        *new electric wheelchair.*

When Savannah hears they're both back—
    Josh *and* Derek—
    she digs around in her shoulder bag,

comes up with these little stars
　　　you stick on your skin,
　　　puts one on each eyelid,
　　　　　and blinks a few times.
　　　She pulls out
　　　two colors of lip gloss.
　　　*Cappuccino or Carnation?* she asks.
　　　*Definitely Cappuccino,* Chen decides,
and Savannah brushes color on her lips,
then turns to go look for Josh and Derek,
assuming, as she always does,
　　　that we'll all follow.
　　　　　And we do.


Am I the only one thinking—wait a minute,
　　　we didn't even introduce ourselves
　　　　　to that girl, we just
　　　　　　　ignored her?
But it's too late—she's picked up her end
　　　of the ramp again—her back is turned
　　　　　to us.


Even with Savannah's finely tuned boy-radar,
it takes us fifteen minutes
to find Josh and Derek.
　　　They're at the snack bar with a boy
　　　　　we don't know, named Carl. Josh has
　　　　　enough snacks for a mini-feast
　　　　　and when we all sit down at the picnic table,
　　　　　he spreads them out. *Wren,* he asks,

*do you still like green gummi bears?*
I say: *No, that was so thirteen of me.*
I don't say: *I like that you remember.*


*There's the new girl,* says Toryn.
She's with her mom now,
    and they're arguing as they walk past.
    She glances at us, lowering her voice,
    but I hear what she says:
        *Mom, will you listen to me for once?*
        *I know I'm going to hate it here.*


    Her mom thinks about it, and says,
    *Give it two weeks.*
    *If you're not happy . . .*


My hands get all damp.


    My heart starts pounding hard.


I can't breathe.


    What's wrong with me?


*I have to go back to the cabin,* I say.
    *Thanks, Josh. See you later.*
    And I walk away.


Toryn follows me: *Did I miss something?* she asks.
    My mouth is so dry I can't answer.
    I walk faster, away from Toryn.

She calls after me.
*What's wrong?*
*Can I do anything?*

*Wren?*

The new girl
hears my name
and jerks around.

Why is she staring at me?

## I've Never Seen Her
### Darra


How many girls my age named Wren can there be? Plus I
remember her picture, and she looks exactly
the same. Older, of course, and different hair,
but it has to be her. Now I really don't want to stay! *Mom, could
we please get back in the car and go home?*
Mom says, *Grandma just wanted you to be
happy! Is that asking so much of you?* How many ways can I tell
her the same thing? I turn away. She goes, *Darra!*
And this girl, Wren, hears my name, and gets
a look, like something just hit her. I see it in slow motion. She
doesn't want to look at me, but she can't help it,
and I can't help staring back. Mom asks,
*Do you know that girl?* I think: *Hello? Remember? She was
in our garage, eavesdropping on everything
we did and said for two nights and a day. She told
the cops where we lived, so Dad got arrested! You know—the one
who ruined our lives?* I say, *No, I've never
seen her before.* (True.) We walk to the car.
Mom gets in, says goodbye, rolls up her window, takes a drink of
her water, and starts off. She has a long drive
ahead of her, and she works the late shift

tonight. I know she has to get going, but this is one of those
times when I really miss Dad. For one thing, he'd
fix our car so the door on my side would open.
I go back to the cabin, step past Wren Abbott and three other girls
in a tight little square by the door.
They look at me like there's some mistake.
Everyone knows you have to have money to go to this camp—who
let *me* in? So, okay, I'm here—now what?
I go in, put my things on a wobbly shelf,
unfold the sheets, and make my bed, like I see everyone else has
already done. The girls who were outside
come in, and K.C. introduces us.
Wren knows my name, I'm sure of it, but she pretends she's never
heard of me. She has a top bunk—from a
certain angle, we can see each other in a mirror
on the wall between our beds. It's so obvious all these girls have been
here before, and have everything all figured out.
For example, my pillow is lumpy—everyone else
apparently knew they should bring a good one from home. I hit
the pillow to break up the lumps,
sit back on my bed, and watch.

## The Tree Was Cold
### Wren

Darra Monson looks at me like she knows who I am.

Is she expecting me to say I remember
      when we were eight years old,
            and kinda-almost met each other?

I shake my head a tiny bit—no,
      I can't do that.

When I heard her and her mom talking,
      I must have remembered their voices
            from somewhere down deep,
            like music or stories you don't quite forget.

A story Dad used to tell me floats up in my mind:
      *Once there was a beautiful tree,*
      *and its leaves all fell to the ground.*
            *The tree looked up—*
            *nothing between it and the sky*
            *but darkness. The tree was cold.*
            *It didn't know*

*new leaves would grow back . . .*
    The story had a happy ending,
    sort of—the tree finds out
    that the leaves it lost
    become part of the new ones.


Darra gets up and walks out of the cabin.
    She doesn't say where she's going.


*That car her mom drives,*
    says Savannah, *did you see it?*
    *I'm surprised it's even running.*
    (How much does Darra hear?)
    *They could at least spray-paint over the rust spots.*


And then I smell spray paint—
    I'm afraid
        I might vomit.
Maybe later I'll find a way to defend Darra,
    but now I'm closing my mouth
        as hard as I can.
    *Wren, you look sick,* says Toryn.
    *I'll be okay,* I manage to answer,
        swallowing hard.


    I *am* okay. I didn't
    throw up. I didn't
    start off the summer
    telling Savannah it's not right
    to make fun of people's
    clothes and cars.

But why
        couldn't I at least say:
        Darra seems nice enough.
        Try to give her a little backup—
                like I'm pretty sure
                she once tried to do for me.

## What Are You Scared Of?
### Darra


I'm skipping out on what K.C. calls cabin time. I find a rock to sit on
in the shade, near the waterfront. Day two.
Watching six kids take their swimming test—
scrawny eight-year-olds trying to pretend they're these big TV
Olympic swimmer dudes. It looks like
they have to jump off the dock and swim
to the rope and back before they can go out to the deep part. The
teacher, Miles, is trying to make this one kid,
Sam, jump in, and it's obvious that
Sam doesn't want to. I bet he's never been away from his mom
before. *Come on, you can do it,*
Miles says. Why does he keep saying that,
when Sam just told him he can't? He's shivering on the dock and
he looks scared to death. Doesn't
Miles know how far away
the water looks to this kid? I used to hate it so much when Dad
scared me and then said, *What are you scared of?*
I learned to never show fear, but now when
someone is afraid, they can't hide it from me. *Sam, how long were*
*you planning to stand there looking at the water?*
Miles asks. He's not being mean, but still,

I feel like telling him: Don't try to talk this kid out of crying—
let him go back to his cabin if he can't
jump off the dock. Finally, Miles
gets in the water. *Trust me. I'm right here*,
he says. Sam holds his nose—he wants to jump, but he's begging,
*Don't make me! I'll go under!*
Miles waits with his arms open
to catch him, and Sam finally jumps into the water, looks around for
Miles, and grabs him, spluttering. *I did it!*
*I did it! I never thought I could,*
*but I did!* That must feel good—to help little kids get up their
nerve to try something they don't think
they can do. Sam climbs out and then
he tries it again—this time he paddles out toward the rope a little,
turning around every couple of feet to see
if Miles is watching. When he gets out
and wraps up in his towel, I give him a thumbs-up. I'm just some girl
he doesn't know, but he grins at me.
I have to take my test in half an hour—
I'm planning to try for the Lifesaving class. I guess I'll go back
to the cabin—if Sam can jump
off the dock, I can face those cabin-girls.

## Swim to the Near Rope
### Wren

We're all heading to the waterfront
    to take our swimming tests
        when Darra comes back to the cabin.
*Wren, why don't you wait for her,* K.C. suggests.
    Darra glances at me: *No, I'm good,* she says.
    She'll be okay—she knows the way.

All six of us are sitting on the dock
    when Darra arrives.
Savannah glances at me, meaning, *Look*
    *at her swimming suit.*
        (I wish I didn't even understand
            that look—
            I don't return it.)

Miles is assistant waterfront director this year.
    He's also the counselor for Boys Cabin Eight—
    good thing I like him, because our two cabins
        will have a lot of activities together.

He welcomes Darra,
>     and she sits on the dock,
>     as far from me as possible.

I ask, *Can I take Lifesaving this year?*
Miles teases me: *Whoa, Wren, aren't you, like, ten years old?*
He knows I'm fourteen—
>     I'm pretty sure he'll let me in.

First we take the easy test, in order to be allowed out on the raft.
>     Miles gives the instructions:
>     *Swim to the near rope and back*
>     *and then tread water for five minutes.*
>     Everyone but Rachel
>         passes that part easily.

To get into Lifesaving,
>     you have to know five different strokes, plus
>     swim half a mile and then
>         dive down, find a brick, bring it up,
>             and swim with it out to the raft.

I can do all my strokes—Miles checks them off.
>     I swim the half mile. *Good,* he says.
>     Now, if I can just get the brick—
>             I did it!

What—?
Why is Darra swimming the half mile?
>     She's trying out for Lifesaving?

We're the only ones
    from our cabin
    to try for this.


She's taking Boating at the same time I am too,
so if we both get into Lifesaving,
that would mean . . .
    almost our whole morning together.


It's not that I don't like her—
    it's just that . . . she knows too much
        about me.


I have to find a way to tell her
    I don't want to talk about
what happened
        without it sounding like
        I'm still
        messed up
        about it.


Because I'm not.
    I got over all that
    long ago.
        Really.
        I'm fine.

## Buddy Board
### Darra

I'm getting into the routine. After lunch every day, we go back to the
cabin for rest hour, and I lie down on my bed facing
the wall. Huh? What's this, sticking out from under
my pillow? A yellow envelope with "Darra" written in perfect girl's
handwriting, all round and even. I try to hide it
and open it at the same time (not too hard because
no one notices me much). At least someone here knows my name.
But who? The card is all sunflowers
and butterflies. My hands shake when
I read the short note inside: *If you don't talk about who I was*
*or how you knew me, I won't talk about*
*you or your dad.* It isn't signed, but I know
who it has to be from. I turn around just enough to look up at Wren
in the mirror, but she doesn't glance down.
Is she going to pretend she didn't write it?

Three hours later, we're walking to the waterfront for free swim, and I
think I might catch Wren's eye, just to nod, Okay,
but she walks ahead with Toryn. It looks like she
doesn't want to talk to me. I try to act cheerful, like I would if I felt
included, but everyone else pairs up,

so when we get to the "buddy board"
(you have to have a buddy before you go in), they're all, *Sorry,*
*Darra, I already have a buddy.* Right next to the
buddy board, there's a glassed-in case with
a list of everyone in the Lifesaving class. It's taken two days for
Miles to post it—I got in! So did Wren, and
one other girl, Jonna. Also five boys, including
Jeremy (the one I met the first day). I want to tell Wren, but her
back is turned to me. Never mind.
She'll find out sooner or later.

A group of little kids crowd in—it must be Boys Cabin Two. I
recognize Sam, and smile at him.
He grabs my arm. *You remember me?*
*You watched me take my test! Will you be my buddy?* Who knew
I could make someone so happy? *Okay,*
I answer, and he gives me a huge smile.
Savannah sees that I'm buddies with an eight-year-old. She
opens her eyes wide and looks at Jeremy
and Derek, nodding her head toward me.
Derek shrugs. Jeremy shoots a smile my way. *Hey, Darra, I would*
*have been your buddy,* he says. Sam pulls
me away, and I say to Jeremy, *It looks like*
*I'm taken.* All I really need is one friend here, and Jeremy would be
a lot better than Sam, but hey, maybe I'll have
two. Sam drags me into the water, instructing me:
*You stand right there, and I'll jump in. Catch me if I get scared.*
He jumps in, swims a few feet, and stands up
smiling. *Now what should we play?* he asks.

## Marco Polo
### Wren


Everyone knows the rules for free swim.
>Stay inside the ropes.
>No cannonballs off the raft.
>No running on the dock.

Miles reminds us:
*You don't have to stick with your buddy all the time,*
>*but don't swim so far apart*
>>*that you can't get back together*
>>*to hold up your hands*
>>*when the whistle blows.*

We all plunge in.
>I swim with Toryn out to the raft and we dive
>>off the diving board.
>>Jeremy and Derek swim out—
>>Savannah won't be far behind.
>>Here she comes now.

There are too many kids on the raft,
>so Miles sends half of us back in, including me.

Darra's in the shallow part, surrounded by little kids
    who holler their heads off whenever
    she yells *Marco!* and swims after them.
    *Polo!* they yell. *Polo! Polo!*,
    swimming away from her, ducking underwater.

She looks happy,
    like she's having so much fun
    she doesn't care about us.
        She tags Meghan's little brother, Sam,
            then dives down
    and pops up somewhere else.
        Sam could break our eardrums
        with his screeching.
        *Marco! Marco!*
    I'm dangling my feet off the dock
    while Darra
        acts like
        an eight-year-old . . .

. . . and it happens again . . . I feel like
    I'm eight years old . . .

    (. . . the warm car
        . . . the gunshot
            . . . the bumpy, dusty car ride
                . . . the dark garage . . .)

Sam swims over to me, grins,
    and grabs my foot.

( . . . grit on the floor of the car.
How far am I
from home?
Do. Not. Move.
Can't breathe . . . )


Sam is laughing, teasing, trying to pull me in.
All the little kids are watching.


Darra swims over and says,
*Want to play?*
And—
my leg flies out.
I kick her—hard
in her right arm.


*Hey! What'd you do that for? It's just a game!*
Four little boys are shouting at me.
Darra doesn't say a word.
I turn away, trying to hide my face,
silently telling my tears—stop it!
The way you might try to command
a disobedient dog.

## Can You Skip Me?
### Darra


Wren's not exactly making it easy for me to avoid talking about "it."
Everyone saw her kick me—they
must think there was a reason.
Jeremy was watching. I saw her talking to him later, and he won't
know there's another whole part
of the story—whatever story she might
have told him. I don't really care, except Mom insists I have to be
here for another week and a day. It would
help to have a friend close to my age,
and Jeremy seems nice. I mean, maybe "friend" would be a long
shot, but I know he doesn't despise me.
Oh well. Six days down. Eight to go.
K.C. does this "one special moment" thing every night before
she turns out the lights. Rachel
says, *I threw my first pot this morning.*
Toryn: *I got a letter from Mom today. Everything's good at home. Dad
got a job.* Savannah starts in, *At two minutes
after one o'clock, I notice Derek looking at me
across the woodwork shop. He sees me looking back and gets
a little smile on his face and we* . . .
She goes on for five minutes, giving

every detail of her "moment." Wren mentions her happy home
like she thinks everybody has one:
*Even though I'm not quite old enough,*
*Miles let me into Lifesaving, and Mrs. Seeger let me call Mom*
*and Dad and Alex to tell them, and they were*
*all cheering on the phone. Alex said he knew*
*I could do it.* I remember Alex, her older brother. Mom said
to leave everything in the car that night,
but I didn't. I kept a little photo album.

I found it under the seat of their car. Alex was ten back then, if I'm
remembering right. I hid the album in the back
of my closet, and I liked to take the pictures out
and look at them. I'd wonder where Wren and Alex were going,
all dressed up, in that one picture. *Darra?* says K.C.
What? It's my turn? *Can you skip me?* I say.
*Nothing special happened today.* But K.C. answers, *No, try to*
*think of something.* It would be pathetic to say,
"A girl in Cabin Six talked to me." Or:
"I played water basketball with Boys Cabin Two." That won't work.
I'll make something up. "My parents got a new car"?
"Parents," that's good. But what if K.C. knows
about Dad? At first, I was sure no one here knew about that, but now,
I come to find out, Mrs. Beams, the head cook,
was Grandma's friend "back in the day."
She said to me, *I'm right here for you if you need anything, honey.*
I blurt out, *Mrs. Beams called me "honey."*
Okay, I know that was dumb.

All the girls laugh—at Mrs. Beams? Or at me? Toryn says, *There's*
*a lot of people she calls honey, Darra.* Including,

it turns out, Dan, the boating director, who has
also worked here forever, and likes Mrs. Beams, or maybe the pizza
she gives him late at night. Or something.
K.C. interrupts just when it starts to get
interesting. *Chen?* she says. *Well, okay, but I'm not sure if
this is special or not* (I thought that about
mine too). *You know how, when you mix
all the colors together, you get brown? Well, I found out that you
can make different shades of brown by adjusting
the amounts of each color.* I don't know how special
that is, but it's interesting. K.C. turns out the lights and we all get
quiet. When she thinks we're asleep, she goes out
to sit on the front steps of the cabin. But no one
is asleep. Meghan whispers across the top bunks to Wren, *Hungry?*
Wren says, *Yeah!* And before long,
there's a sneaky little party going on.

## Block and Parry
### Wren


Lifesaving is the last class every morning,
    the hour right before lunch.
    It's cold when we dive in the water.
Four laps of freestyle, two butterfly, three backstroke,
    fifteen minutes treading water.

Now Miles is demonstrating this thing called
    "block and parry." *I need someone
    to get in the water with me,* he says.
    Jeremy took the class last year—
    he didn't pass, but he knows more than the rest of us,
    so he gets in the water and acts like he's drowning.

Miles swims toward him as if he's going to rescue him,
    and right when it looks like he's got him in
        a carrying position,
            Jeremy twists around
                and lunges,
            getting Miles in a headlock,
                pushing him down
                underwater.

Whoa, Jeremy—don't drown the teacher!

But then we see
    Miles bob up
        smiling,
            a few yards away.

His point: you might think
    your victim will be
        grateful to be rescued,
            but if you're
            not careful,
the person can panic, get away,
    and come after you—
    you can end up
        needing to be rescued
        yourself.

*We don't want a double drowning,* Miles says.

### Shouldn't You Two Be Partners?
  *Darra*


This Wren thing is getting harder. Like in Lifesaving class: *Shouldn't*
*you two be partners? You're about the same size—*
*Jonna is way taller.* And I'm thinking,
*Well, yeah, I would be partners with Wren, but, see, my dad*
*kinda kidnapped her one time,*
*and she might not like me too much.*
I don't know what Wren says if people ask her. It wouldn't be
so bad if Lifesaving was our only class
together, but we have Boating together too.
And rest hours, and bedtimes in the cabin. She gets letters from home
*every day.* Including the first day we were
here, which means someone wrote her a letter
before she left home! She puts them all in a little box on the shelf by
her bed, right next to my shelf, in the space between
our two bunks. At first I didn't pay much attention,
but yesterday, she showed Toryn a picture her mom sent—and now
I'm thinking about her family.
What does her brother look like
after all this time? In all the pictures of him and Wren together, I
saw how happy they both looked. Making

a big snowman, or washing a car (Alex
scrubbing with a soapy sponge, Wren rinsing with a hose). I wondered
if they were posing for those pictures. It didn't
seem like it; they looked like two good friends.

## Like Sisters or Cousins
### Wren

Toryn says, *Wren, seems like you've changed.*
    *Is everything good with you?*
    She's waiting for me outside the shower house
    to walk back to the cabin together.

Toryn has been my best friend at camp for four years.
    Lots of people, when they first meet us,
        ask if we're sisters
        or cousins or something.
    But even to her, I've never talked about
        "what happened."
        I haven't told her
        how I know—or don't know—
            Darra.

*I can't say what it is,* she says.
    *You're quieter. You've always been*
    *friendly to everyone, know what I mean?*
    *Is something going on, like maybe*
        *your parents are getting divorced?*

Her voice shakes a little when she says that—
     is there something in her life
     she wants to tell me about?

*No, I'm good,* I say.
*How about you?* She doesn't answer right away.
     *Um, yeah. There was some hard stuff*
     *at home this year,* she finally says.
     *Dad lost his job. I didn't think*
     *I'd be able to come back to camp.*
     *Then Mom took out a loan to pay for it,*
     *and they had a big fight about that.*

Some people think everyone at this camp
     has to be rich, but it's not true. I wait
     to see if Toryn is going to say something
     about a divorce. She doesn't.

We're almost back to the cabin.
     We slow down so we can keep talking.
     *Is that why you can only come*
     *for two weeks this year?*
          She nods.
     *Things might get better*
     *now that your dad got a job,* I say.
     It's all I can think of, not much help.
     She says, *Yeah, maybe.*
     *But I don't want to leave*
          *next Saturday.*

Saying goodbye is always the worst part of camp.

## Sam's Table
### *Darra*

*Darra is sitting with Boys Cabin Two?* By now everyone
is used to it. It started the day I played
Marco Polo with the little kids. When
I didn't know where to sit in the dining hall, Sam saw that I was
looking for a table and he jumped up:
*Darra! Sit with me! Sit here!*
Like I was the coolest friend a kid could have. I kept searching
for someone my age to sit with, but all
the tables were either empty or reserved—
you know how people can make you feel like something is saved for
other people, and even if they don't say who,
you know it isn't you? That's how it was.
So I sat at Sam's table. Impressed his friends. Who knows if Wren
and the rest of Cabin Eight even noticed,
that first time, but by now they do.
Maybe I'll try sitting with them, one of these meals. Wren Abbott—
as Sam would say—is not the boss of me.
Four more days until I can leave if I want to.

*I Was Thinking*
    *Wren*


I hear Darra telling K.C.,
    *I only have four days left, anyway.*
    *My mom promised*
        *I didn't have to stay*
        *more than two weeks.*

I glance over at them.
Darra doesn't look at me.
K.C. asks, *Are you sure?*
    *I don't know, somehow*
    *it just doesn't seem right—*
    *you paid for four weeks,*
    *and you only want to stay for two?*

An idea sneaks into the back of my mind—a way to turn this
    into something good for Toryn.
        I wonder if they'd do it.


I know I should try
    to convince Darra to stay.
    I know this isn't fair. It isn't nice.

We haven't given her much of a chance
    to fit in
    and be happy here.


But I'm thinking of Toryn (I tell myself)
    as I walk out of the cabin,
        past K.C. and Darra, and go straight
           to the camp office.
   *Mrs. Seeger,* I say,
    *Could I talk to you?* She motions me in.
    *I know this might not be any of my business,*
    *but you know how much Camp Oakwood*
    *means to Toryn. She's been coming*
    *here since she was seven years old, and everybody*
    *loves her. Now she has to leave,*
    *and she's having a hard time with that.*
    *So I was thinking . . .*


Even as I start to say it, the whole idea starts fading
    into bad-idea land. (*It just doesn't seem right,*
        as K.C. said.)
My half-finished sentence hangs in the air.
    (What *was* I thinking, anyway?)


Mrs. Seeger leans back in her chair.
    *What is it, Wren?*


I was thinking (I don't say) . . . wouldn't it be nice
    if Darra Monson got back in that rusty car
    on Saturday, went home—
        and I never had to face her again.

Mrs. Seeger is giving me her it's-okay-you-can-tell-me look.
    She probably guesses
    this isn't all about Toryn.

I was going to ask:
What if someone goes home early and
    the money they paid for those weeks
        can't be refunded —
    can someone else come
        (or stay) in their place?

But when I picture a car door closing
    next Saturday morning,
        it's Darra
    I see crying as she leaves.

*Never mind, Mrs. Seeger,* I say.

## I've Decided
### Darra

Mom writes that she'll call on Thursday. I have to be at the office when
she calls, ready to tell Mrs. Seeger
what I've decided. The letter says,
*I'd have to get the day off, and I should take the car in first. I
need to get a new battery.* I wish she'd have
the car painted, but she thinks the battery
is more important. She says she'll try to get the door fixed. She heard
about a place she might be able to afford.
I think: How long have I been climbing
across the driver's seat because that door hasn't opened since Dad
left, unless I kick it exactly right? And then I think:
I could stay at camp another two weeks if I want to.

I knew the my-dad's-a-CEO-what's-yours? conversation would come
up sooner or later. Usually I can avoid
answering. ("It's hard to explain," I say.)
I lie if I have to. ("My dad's self-employed. He works at home
designing computer software.") But today
when Savannah asks what my father does,
in that second it takes me to decide what to say, Wren interrupts, and I
don't have to answer. *Savannah,* she asks,

88

*what do they make at your dad's company?*
I'm pretty sure she did that on purpose. No one noticed how she turned
the conversation away from me. Savannah
finishes bragging about her dad. Then Wren
talks about her mom, who teaches college—it sounds like she goes off
on a lot of interesting trips, but Wren doesn't
talk about that too long. She changes the subject
before anyone asks me any more about Dad, helping me avoid the
question I hate most. I look at her.
If I leave on Saturday, I'll never
get to know her—the girl from back then, those two days on TV,
trapped in our garage. But more: who she is now.
I'm going to tell Mrs. Seeger I've decided to stay.

## Drown Last
### Wren


Miles teaches us this new game
    called Drown Last.
      It sounds like some kind of reality show
      where everyone is trying to drown each other
         and be the last one alive.

We all have to dive off the raft on the deep side,
and then everyone tries to rescue everyone else,
while trying not to be rescued—
    that is, carried to a place on the rope
    that Miles has marked as "Home."
I'm dreading this—I'm the smallest one here.

*There's only one rule*, Miles says.
*If you tap someone three times, it means,*
    *"You win, I'm giving up."*
    *Then you have to stop fighting and let them take you in.*

He wants us to learn what it feels like
    to rescue someone
        who panics so much

they can't understand
you're trying to help them.

I know I'll be the first one "rescued,"
but I might as well try
to come up with a plan.
My only possibilities
are Jonna and Peter
(besides Darra).

I do not want to play this.

But when Miles blows his whistle, we all dive in.

I look around. Good—
I'm nowhere near Jeremy.
He goes straight for this kid Matt,
who is smaller than Derek.

Derek goes after Tyler,
who is smaller
than both Matt and Jeremy.

I look around for Jonna. She's bigger than me,
but I might be stronger.
I'd have to sneak up from behind
and get her in a hold
before she sees me coming.

Oh.
That's her over there—going after Peter.

What now? Darra is the only one left. She
   doesn't want to fight me
   any more than I want to fight her.
   But there's no other choice.

Slowly, warily, we swim toward each other.

## I Don't Surface
### Darra

One of us will have to dive underwater and start this. What
is Wren planning to do? Maybe, like me,
she wants to stay out of everyone's way
as long as she can. It looks like she's not in the mood
for this either, but I guess she's decided
to fight it out with me, since Jeremy already
has Matt in a cross-chest carry, and if we're still in the game, he would
most likely come after one of us next. Matt
fights hard, but Jeremy gets him to Home
and gives Miles a thumbs-up (just like I used to do when Dad
saw me do something good). Jeremy looks
over at Wren and me, treading water, watching
each other—okay, this is it. I tuck into a surface dive, trying to be
quick and smart, because I think Wren is
stronger than I am. I swim behind her—
it's murky down here—grab her legs, turn her around, get her in
a hold, and start swimming hard,
carrying her toward Home.

She sucks in a breath and pushes against me. She *is* strong. I'd
better swim faster. Halfway to Home, she

breaks free, turns, lunges at me, gets me
in a hold I can't break out of, no matter how hard I twist. If I try
to kick my way underwater, maybe I can
take her down with me. It works—she
releases me. Now we're facing each other underwater. She tries to
grab me. I pull away, then reach for her arms,
but she gets my hair, pulls me toward her,
and kicks hard to surface. Only—I don't surface—I stay
under. She's holding me down
and I can't get away. I tap her three times—
she won't let me up—Wren! I don't care if she pulls out
a fistful of my hair—I need air!
I tap harder. Let go! But she doesn't—
she keeps pushing me down. I pull my legs up, twist toward her. Out of
someplace deep inside myself, I explode—
I kick Wren—my knees to her stomach.
And she lets me go. When I come up, Miles is blasting away on his
whistle. He plunges into the water,
swims out to us. I'm gasping for breath.
Is Wren—crying? *Darra,* says Miles. *Over here, out of her way.*
*Wren—swim back to the raft.*
*Take it easy,* he tells us both. *It's okay.*
He looks back and forth from Wren to me like he doesn't know if
it's safe to leave either of us alone.
*I tapped her . . . three times . . .* I say.
*Never mind,* Miles says. *Jeremy—could you swim in with Darra? I
need to make sure Wren is okay.*
Jeremy looks like he's proud
to be asked, but I don't want him to see me right now. *You could
let me swim in alone,* I tell him. *I know,* he says,
swimming beside me, looking away.

## Waves Roll In
### Wren

On the edge of the raft, looking out at the lake,
    I wipe my hands across my face.
    Again. Again.
Miles drapes a towel over my shoulders.

Small waves roll in.
    Two ducks swim by,
    the male's green neck shimmering.

A little ways out, a fish
    arcs into the air,
    disappears back into the water.

It's hard to start
    breathing again.
    That anger, that terror—where did it come from?

    The knot of *what happened back then*—
    Darra kicked me right at its center.

I couldn't let go of her hair. Could not.
　　Could not let her up.

Afterwards, out there in the water,
　　Darra told Miles
　　　　she tapped me
　　　　　　three times.
　　I didn't feel it—
　　　　didn't know
　　　　　　I was sobbing.

Like nightmares I used to have—
　　going downhill
　　　　faster
　　　　　　faster
in a car where I couldn't see
　　the driver.

*Are You All Right?*
  *Darra*


I didn't want to kick Wren. I know how it feels. One time, Dad
kicked Archie, and when I leaned down
to pick Archie up, he kicked *me* out of the way.
Miles must be giving Wren time to calm down. She's turned
around, facing the lake. He calls from the raft:
*Drown Last is over for today. Everyone out
of the water.* We look at each other as we spread our towels on
the sand. Jonna finally asks, *Darra,
what happened?* I could tell her all
about it. I could whisper it just to her. (I picture myself going into the
dining hall: *Sorry, Sam, I'm sitting with Jonna
and the Cabin Nine girls.*) The words are right
in my mouth—*Wren totally lost control.* I could start this big news
story in my own words before it gets going
another way—*Darra made Wren cry.*


I stop myself. I say, *I guess Wren got a stomach cramp and then
Miles jumped in to make sure she was okay.*
No one's convinced. *It looked like you
were about to Drown First,* Jeremy says, trying to lighten this up. He
was looking right at us when I finally


97

surfaced. *I got water in my nose,* I tell him,
*but I was okay.* Out on the raft, Wren's back is still turned.
I breathe deep and call out to Miles,
*Can I go back to my cabin?*
He answers, *Okay, but come back if K.C.'s not there.* He knows it
is K.C.'s free hour—she'll probably be there.
When I arrive, she's sitting out on the steps.
*Hey, Darra,* she says. She looks up at my face. *Are you all right?*
And that's when I know I'm not.
My head hurts where Wren pulled my hair.
My throat is burning. K.C. says, *Why don't you get that wet suit off
and put on some dry clothes. Then come out
and sit in the sun with me.* So I do.
Now I'm sitting here with K.C., going over the whole thing again
in my mind. The water is always
colder down deep than it is at the top.

## I Want to Make Sure
### Wren

I'm breathing okay again,
    ready to dive in
    and swim back to shore,
but Miles gives me a ride
    in the rowboat that's tied to the raft.

*I don't know*
    *what hap—*
        My voice cracks.

Miles keeps rowing.
He says, *Don't worry about it.*
    *I'm surprised, though.*
    *Has anything like that ever happened*
        *to you before?*

I shake my head no. (Not exactly.)

I heard him tell Darra she could go to the cabin—
    it looks like she's not coming back.

First—I can't face the other kids,
    sitting on towels on the sand,
        staring their questions at me.
And—this takes me by surprise—
    I want to make sure
        Darra's okay.

Miles reads my mind:
    *Why don't you head back to your cabin.*

Darra and K.C.
    are sitting together
    on the front steps.

Darra puts up her hand for a fist-bump.
    She smiles a little.
        She's okay—
            she's making sure I am.
And—
    I'm glad she's here.
    That's all.
        I'm glad.

I meet her fist.
    I give her
    a small smile back
    as I go into the cabin
    to change.

## In the Sun
### Darra

K.C. goes in. Wren comes out and sits with me. Do we
both know we'll be friends now? Everyone
else is still at their last morning classes.
I start thinking about what happened when we were
little kids, both of us so scared
and neither of us knowing
what to do or who to ask for help. For a while, we're quiet
as we let our hair dry in the sun. *You used to*
*have braids,* I finally say. She nods.
Tim, the maintenance man, goes by on his four-wheeler, waves as
he drives past. *Yeah—with those beads*
*that clicked when I moved,* she answers.
*One time,* I tell her, *I tried to get Mom to put beads in my hair.* We
smile a little at that. After a while,
Wren says, *Sorry, Darra.* And I say,
*It's okay.* And then, *I'm sorry too.* (I'm sorry I know you ate
cat food. I'm sorry I wasn't more help.)
Wren turns to look at me—this look
like she's never seen me before. I ask, *Were you cold?*
I'm asking two questions at once,

and I hear her double answer:

*Yes. I was.* Then, *Sit with me at lunch?* she asks. *Today is pizza.*
That will be good. *Would it be okay,*
I ask, *if Sam sits with us too?*

*Slideshow of Memories*
  *Wren*


It's like I'm seeing Darra
    for the first time.

For six years, I had this picture
    in my mind, just from hearing her voice—
black hair and dark eyes, I thought,
        not Asian or Hispanic,
        some kind of dark-haired
        white person—Italian, maybe.

The first day of camp, when I figured out who she was,
    I couldn't believe it—red hair
        and green eyes?

I look at her
    sitting across from me at the lunch table,
        sunburned nose, freckles.
            She tucks a strand of hair behind her ear.
            It falls right back into her eyes.

All she says is, *Wren, want some water?*
    and this whole slideshow of memories
    comes flashing out of somewhere
    I barely know
        is still there.

    *Yes, I do—thanks, Darra.*

## Old Shipwrecks
### Darra


So much has happened since I decided not to leave. Yesterday I
went on a field trip in a glass-bottom boat
on Lake Superior. We could look down and see
old shipwrecks deep underwater. It was interesting, but I kept
picturing the storms, and the ships
in those last hours or minutes. I looked
at things the crew couldn't save—they must have been thinking
they might get rescued. There were pictures of some
of the people who drowned. I didn't look for too long.


It's the end of the first two-week session. Wren is telling me about
a major Camp Oakwood tradition: Tonight
is Toryn's last night at camp, and all the girls
in Cabin Eight go with her to find a stone in the creek, at that
place it flows under the bridge. Toryn
brings it back to the cabin, and K.C.
gets out a fine-point blue marking pen for a ceremony where each girl
writes something on the stone. *Like,*
*something nice about Toryn?* I ask.

Wren nods. *Or a wish, or a private joke.* She writes "Mom and Dad"
and draws a heart around it. I don't get it,
but it seems to mean something to Toryn.
I don't know Toryn very well. I think hard. My first night here, she did
introduce herself when everyone else
was ignoring me. When the stone
comes to me, I find an empty space, and write in small letters: "You
rock, Toryn." Now the whole camp is heading
to the campfire circle. The kids who are leaving
will place their stones on top of ones already there. You can still see
the writing on stones from last year. *Each year,*
*the ones on the bottom sink into the sand,*
Mrs. Seeger says. *We've been placing these stones for sixty years. The*
*circle we gather around, and the fire we're lighting,*
*represent the friendship of Camp Oakwood campers,*
*past, present, and future.* So that means when Grandma was a girl,
she put a stone on this circle, and it's buried down
there? Cool. Only—does Mrs. Seeger have to make
all this sound like the Pledge of Allegiance? Toryn puts her stone on
the circle, and comes back to sit with Wren.
They link arms—I think they might start crying.
I feel a little left out, but then Sam sees me, and he leaves the
Cabin Two boys and comes and squishes in
between me and Wren. I look over the top
of his head at Wren, and she shoots me a smile. It's no news
to anyone that Sam has a little crush
on me. His hair smells like the lake.
We sing a bunch of songs that everyone but me seems to know. I
hum along, joining in wherever I can.

*Miss Mary Mack, Mack, Mack,* they sing,
*all dressed in black, black, black*—it goes on, all about how she asked
her mother for fifty cents to see some elephants
jump over a fence. It's silly, but, I'll admit it, fun.

***Introductions***
*Wren*


Toryn's mom (and dad—that's good)
    picked her up an hour ago,
    and there's already someone else
    sitting on her bed. It's okay,
    it's Mikki—it's just that
    the changeover always happens
        too fast.


Two of the new girls,
    Mikki and Sylva,
    were here last year—
    I'm glad they're back.


And there's this other girl, a friend of Savannah's
    named Skye.
    Savannah tries to get Darra
    to switch beds so Skye
    can be next to her.


*No!* I say. *Stay here, Darra!*
    Savannah goes, *What—you two are tight now?*

*What's up with that? Derek said*
*you almost killed each other*
     *the other day.*

Darra says, *Derek doesn't know*
     *everything.* (From the look on Savannah's face,
     that has never occurred to her.)

Mikki and Sylva glance at each other,
     taking everything in:
     Darra and I almost killed each other.
     (Or maybe not.)

Savannah and Derek?

Who is this new girl, Darra,
     standing up to Savannah?

K.C. starts to introduce everyone.
     Maybe she missed it—
     we've pretty much already
          done that ourselves.

## Prisoner's Base
### Darra

I'm glad Mom put this in a clean envelope--a letter from Dad
in today's mail. Sounds like he's doing okay.
I'm sitting outside the cabin reading it when
Sam comes running over with his session two schedule. I got
accepted as an assistant teacher
in Nature Crafts, which he's taking,
so I'll be seeing him a lot. He's all excited about going out to pick up
acorns and sticks. Then Chen comes to tell me
about *another* Camp Oakwood tradition.
(There are so many of them!) Apparently, after we get back from
dinner on the second night of session two,
there's always a game of Prisoner's Base.
One team is Girls Cabin Eight and Boys Cabin Nine, and the
other is Boys Cabin Eight and Girls
Cabin Nine. It's this huge thing—
we meet Boys Cabin Nine for a strategy session at a table
set up like a guarded fortress. If "enemies"
walk by, everyone stops talking.
Jeremy is on our side and Derek isn't. Chen says, *You know I went
to a lot of trouble to keep our plans secret. If anyone
tells someone on the other side our strategy before*

*the game, that person* (meaningful look at Savannah) *will be left out
of the pizza party afterwards.* Part of the tradition
is that all four cabins get together after the game
for a party—with dancing—so Chen is making a serious threat to
Savannah. Here's how the game works: Each side
marks off a place at one end of the field to be
their "prison" and if someone catches you, you have to go into the
prison and stay there until someone
from your team tags you and sets you free.
(I wish there'd been rules like this when Wren was in our garage—
maybe it would have helped me get her out.)
The "prisoners" make a chain, everyone
holding hands, and then the whole chain stretches out on the field and
as long as one of them has a foot in the prison, someone
on their team can touch anyone in the chain and free them
all. So—in the middle of this game, I start thinking, what if Dad came
here and learned how to do this, and then when he
had to go back, he could make a chain with the other
prisoners, like fifty men holding hands, and the chain would go back
into his cell, but one man would stick a hand
out through a window—only how would I
reach that hand? I'd throw a ball on a long string, and they'd pull in
the string and pass the ball hand to hand
to Dad and he'd be like, *Yay! Go Darra!*
Everyone's cheering—I freed a bunch of people? I'm back here again,
and it's Jeremy lifting me off my feet,
spinning me around—like Dad used to do.

### Circle Spiral Dancing
#### Wren

You wouldn't think Josh
    would enjoy dancing,
        but he's crazy good!
He rolls his chair in circles,
    shaking his hair, then slows down
        and keeps on dancing
            with his arms and eyes.
We've been having so much fun,
    I didn't notice Jeremy and Darra over there.
        I guess I shouldn't be surprised—
It's just that everyone has always
    paired me up with Jeremy,
        even though it isn't like that—
        Alex and I have known him for most of our lives,
            so I'm Jeremy's
            best friend's
            little sister.
Josh notices me watching them
    and wheels on over there, so now it's him and me
        and Jeremy and Darra, and Chen joins in,
            and Miles and K.C., all dancing

in a circle, in a spiral, to the center
    of the room
and back.


Why is Skye standing
    by herself outside the circle—
        where's Savannah?
        Um—where's Derek?
Darra reaches out to Skye,
    draws her in to join the rest of us.
        Now here comes Mikki, here comes Sylva.
        Jonna. Carl. Two new boys in Cabin Nine.
This is what I love about Camp Oakwood.
    We've all left home and school behind,
        and we can be whoever we want to be.
            Here, I'm not the girl-who-gets-her-homework-done.
        I'm Wren. I love to dance.
            And Darra's dancing too.
    Mrs. Beams brings out the pizza.
        Mushroom, pepperoni, extra cheese.
            Derek and Savannah come back in
        before K.C. and Miles even notice that they're gone.
There's ice cream in the freezer
and we eat it all.
        The moon and stars are brilliant
            when we walk back to our cabins.

## I Hold the Letter
### Darra

Last night I dreamed that Dad came home. He walked in and Mom
walked out, leaving me standing there
in my own house, not knowing whether
I should follow Mom or stay with Dad. Then today a letter came
from Dad, and the first thing I saw was the note
Mom enclosed: *I didn't read his letter to you,*
*but he wrote to me too, so I know what it says. When you get home,*
*we'll talk about it.* Right there, I knew
something was about to change. I was sitting
on my bunk. All around me, girls were talking, teasing, laughing—and
I felt the same way I did on the first day, like
I was in a foreign country where I don't speak
the language. I tried to take the letter and slip out, but K.C. noticed
me, so I told her I was going to the big rock
by the waterfront. She understands—I need
to be alone. Now I hold the letter in my hand, trying to feel the
weight of it before I read it. It isn't too heavy.
And it isn't light. Dad says: *I'm getting out*
*in October. I'll get up to see you as soon as I find someone with a car.*
I want to see him—of course I do—but . . .
I don't know . . . my life is okay like it is.

## My Mind Is Spinning
### Wren


Mrs. Seeger calls me to the office
to tell me Mom and Dad want me
    to call home. I ask why.
    *They didn't say,* she says.


Mom tells me all about their weekend,
what they had for dinner, how much
they miss me. Then—*I'll get Dad,* she says.


What kind of news is this,
    that Mom wants Dad
        to tell me?


*It's about West Monson, Wren,* he says.
*We received a victim notification call*
    *to let us know he'll be*
        *released in ninety days.*


Wait—I'm a victim? Who says?
Does Darra get this phone call too?

My mind is spinning
around Dad's soothing voice:

*We thought we should let you know,*
*even though we can't see any way*
*this could affect you*
*at this point in your life.*

## Maybe It's Time
### Darra


I don't want to talk about Dad's letter, at least not yet, but when
I get to Boating, Wren looks like
she knows something's wrong.
I try to avoid the whole thing: *What did your dad and mom*
*want you to call home for?* I ask. She looks
away from me, out at the lake. *Oh, nothing,*
she says. *I mean, nobody at home is sick or anything. Look—I saw*
*swans in that same place yesterday.* She points
to a pair of swans, closer to shore than usual.
*I know where their nest is, at least I think I do, over there just past the*
*point. Let's tell Dan we want to be partners*
*on the rowing trip tomorrow, and I can*
*show them to you, and . . .* She's talking faster and faster, like a car
with a distracted driver, and I'm also
thinking about something else, so I
just answer, *Sure.* I barely notice how nice it is to see our names on
Dan's sign-up sheet together, how
no one even comments on it, like
everyone knows we're friends, so of course we'll be partners on the
trip. Now we're all listening to the
water safety rules, my mind flashing

back and forth from *Wear your life jacket at all times* to the news
Dad gave me in his letter. What does Mom
want to talk about when I get home? *If you*
*hear thunder, even in the distance, get off the water.* What does she
think about this? What if Dad wants me
to live with him? Where will he live?
*Don't row near the channel. Swans may be in the rushes—they went*
*in there this morning, and I think they*
*have a nest.* Wren glances at me. So much
for that plan. *Bring a jacket. Even if it's hot here, it can get cold out*
*on the water when the wind blows.*
The boat trip might be a good chance for
a long conversation. Maybe it's time for Wren and me to
talk about "it." Each of us knows
our own part of the story—what if
we could put the pieces all together and step back to have a look
at the whole thing? *Does anyone have*
*any questions?* Dan asks. Yes—I have
a lot of questions. For Wren. How did you get out? What was it like for
you, hiding in the boat in the dark
with nothing to eat? Did you think my
dad shot your mom? Did you know I knew you were in there? *Wren,*
I say, as we walk back to the cabin, *do you think*
*it's time for us to talk about—what happened?*

*I Begin*
   *Wren*


I didn't answer Darra yesterday,
    but I've been thinking
    about what she said—
        and she's right,
        it is time.

Now we're sitting together in the boat.
    I'm rowing.
    Darra's facing me
    and we find ourselves
    out in the middle of the lake.

Small waves lap against the boat.

The swans swim out from the channel,
        raise and dip
        their necks.

I begin.
    *I was a happy little girl*
        *wearing a pink dress . . .*

## It Smelled Like—Dad
### Darra

Wren talks. I listen. I only interrupt once. When she describes the
sweatshirt she found, and says, *It smelled*
*like West,* she spits out his name. *Wesst.*
I stop her. *Wren. It smelled like—Dad.* When I was a little girl
I loved my dad just like she loved hers.
I was mad when they arrested him.
Does that surprise her? I wonder if Wren might think I was
grateful to her, or that I should be, even now.
Does she think you can't love a dad who yells
at you or even hits you? She probably does think that, but it's not
true. And if she doesn't understand that,
she might think she did me a favor, getting
him out of our house. Out of my life. I've always wanted Dad in
my life. Can she get that? When I say *Dad,*
she pulls up the oars and looks out at the water
like she's rethinking something that started back then with the
gunshot she heard (Dad didn't
have a gun) and got bigger and
bigger, the whole time she was so scared in the back of the car,
and in the boat, and running down the road.
*My father is not a monster,* I say.

## Was It a Good Thing?
### Wren

Would it be better
to have a mean dad,
or not to have a dad at all?

That was the question
that tormented me when I was little.
Was it a good thing
West Monson got arrested,
or would his little girl,
named Darra,
be really sad about it?

Was there any reason
that whole thing happened
to me?
Were Darra and Stacey
and Archie
safer
after West was gone?

I told myself
what I had to believe: Yes. They were.

    Now Darra is telling me
      I'm wrong.

## Gentle Waves
### Darra

The swans separate and swim around us as Wren finishes her story. I
have questions I'll ask later, but for now
I simply listen to what happened on that second
morning. *I've always wondered how you got out,* I say. *I never knew
a little kid could fit through a pet door.*
She looks like she's back there right now.
*And you walked to the Amish farm—I saw that on the news.* She
nods, and goes on. *A little dog came to the fence
and sniffed at me. It ran off and came back
with Katie, a girl about my age. When she saw how scared I was,
she got her mom. There was a boy named
John. A baby, Anne. The dad was Amos. They
took me to a phone, and brought me back and fed me. I waited there in
that warm kitchen for Mom and Dad and Alex.
The police came and asked me where you lived.
I almost told them, but when I thought about your family—I didn't. The
girl, Katie, pointed to the way I'd come. Then
one of the police detectives got a big idea:
"We'll drive down that road until we smell a skunk."* Now our boat
is rocking on the gentle waves. Wren
stops rowing and we rest here for a while

to give ourselves a chance to take each other's stories in
and put the pieces into place. Everything
is turning upside down. I look at Wren—
so much to think about. If it's true that she didn't lead the
police to our house like I've always
thought she must have, and if she lost
her shoe and Bilbo got it when she tried to roll under the garage
door, that means— *No one,* I say, *has been lying
to me. None of what happened was your fault.*

## Buddies
### Wren


We get back in the middle of free swim
    and since everyone else
    is already in the water,
        I figure I'll be Darra's buddy.

But it turns out I have competition—
    Sam
        has been waiting patiently
        by the buddy board for Darra
        and she can't say no,
        especially when she hears his news.
    He's practically exploding:
    *I passed! I passed my test! I can swim to the raft!*

Luckily, there's this thing where
    if everyone else is already buddied up,
    the last three people
        can be buddies.

So Darra and I
    swim out to the raft with Sam.

His Cabin Two friends
stand behind the rope,
cheering like he's just won
a gold medal.

*You Know. What Happened.*
   *Darra*


I can't believe it's the end of the third week already. If
I could stay the whole six weeks, I would.
I don't know who has changed—me or
the other people here, but it seems like a different place. I
found out something about Wren and Jeremy
that took me by surprise. Jeremy knows
what happened to Wren when she was eight. When she told
me that, she said, *I haven't told him it was*
*your dad. You can tell him if you want to.*
His family and Wren's have been friends for ten years. Her mom
has a cousin who knew his dad—that's how
they met. Jeremy got to be friends with Alex,
and then Wren. They started coming to camp together. Wren says she'd
be okay with it, if Jeremy and I want to
talk about what happened back then.
I know I want to. Jeremy and I are—I don't know—whatever you call
a boy and a girl who spend a lot of time
together without admitting how they
feel about each other. Today we're on an all-day hike, near the
end of a long climb up a hill to a waterfall
and I tell Jeremy about Dad. I wait for him

to be shocked—most people wouldn't get past the word "police."
Jeremy just says: *Oh.* And keeps walking. At first
I think he doesn't understand how big
a deal it is for me to tell him. But then I look over at his face and
I know that's not it. More like, he's trying
not to let me see how much he cares.
After a few minutes, he says, *Let's sit down on this log. They'd
wait at the waterfall if we got too far behind. Darra,*
he asks, *did Wren tell you how her mom's cousin
met my dad?* I shake my head no, and Jeremy gets quiet. *Come
on—how?* I ask, but he doesn't answer
right away. He seems to be thinking about what
to tell me. *They met in prison, Darra. Dad was getting out and
he knew it would be hard to find a job.*
*Wren's mom's cousin told him to look
up Mr. Abbott, and he did, and Mr. Abbott saw past my dad's arrest
and gave him a job washing school buses.*
*Me and Wren and Alex have been tight since
before Wren got—you know.* What is the word? "Kidnapped"? Dad
didn't know she was in the car, so that's not it. "You
know." "What happened." We use the words we have.

### Like We've Been Taught
#### Wren


We're playing Drown Last again.

Miles says, *I'll be on the raft.*
    *Wren, I want you to guard*
        *from the dock.*

(He's afraid I'll lose control again.)

I'm standing here thinking about
    who each person will try to rescue first,
    and what the winning strategy will be.

Jeremy and Derek will get Tyler and Peter.
Matt will start with Darra or Jonna
    and then come back for the other one
        while Jeremy and Derek fight it out together
        and whichever one is left
        will take Matt
            and win.

Miles blows his whistle. I watch
the game begin.

Whoa—what's this?
Jeremy, going after Darra?
She puts up a fight—
arms flailing, feet kicking,
lots of splashing around—
but it doesn't last long.
Jeremy holds Darra
carefully, gently,
carrying her Home
just like we've been taught.

And then—
he stays with her,
checks to make sure
she's okay.
He's not all who-can-I-get-next.

Jeremy cares
about Darra.

## The Watching Rock
### Darra

It seems innocent enough to me: it's free time, we want to talk, and I
tell Wren and Jeremy about the rock
I sit on sometimes when I want to think.
They laugh. Jeremy puts his arm around me. *For a minute, I thought
you were* inviting *me to the Watching Rock!*
He emphasizes "inviting" in a way that makes
Wren laugh. One more in-joke about Camp Oakwood history. I
don't get upset about this now—I just ask them
to explain. *When we were in the junior cabins,*
Wren says, *everyone thought you were way cool if you knew
what the counselors talked about when they were
alone. We'd sneak out at night and go to that rock.*
Jeremy jokes, *Spying on the counselors might be what taught me how
to talk so sweet to girls.* Wren laughs, and Jeremy
goes on, *We were so quiet! But then they heard us
calling it the Watching Rock, and after that it was impossible for us to
get out of our cabins at night. Anyway, let's go there.
Wren can be our chaperone.* We laugh, but we have
something serious to talk about. It turns out Wren knows Dad will get
out of prison in October (unless he messes up
between now and then). I'm not as happy about

that as I should be. We walk to the rock and sit down. Wren takes her
shoes off and dangles her feet in the water.

I start the conversation with a question:

*Jeremy, do you remember what your dad was like when he got out?*

They both guess why I'm asking. Jeremy says,

*I was just a little kid, Darra, but I remember*
*he was pretty crazy at first.* Wren says, *He must have been scared of*
*whether he'd fit back in.* Jeremy nods and says,

*I've seen a few of his friends when they first*
*get out. They come to him for help, and he helps if he can. If there*
*is something he can do for your dad, Darra,*
*he'll do it. Maybe he'll give him a job—Dad*
*has his own auto body shop now.* (My dad could paint cars—without
stealing them.) Wren's not so sure. She turns to
look at me. *That could be good. But, Darra,*
*if he's like he was—or if he's worse than before—don't let anyone*
*tell you he has to be part of your life.*
*Not your mom. Not him. You make that call.*

Jeremy adds, *It's been—what—six years? No way of knowing*
*until you see him if he's changed for better*
*or worse. It can go either way. And it's true,*
*what Wren said. If he got home and didn't treat you right, I know she'd*
*have your back—and so would I. I'll have my license*
*in four months. I'll be less than an hour's drive away.*

Whoa—he's got that figured out already! How long have I been
holding in the breath that I let out?

Wren reaches over and grabs my hand.

*I'm not playing with you, Darra. Don't forget—I was there.*

I answer, *I was there too. I won't forget.*
*I'm not going back to the way it was.*

## One More Thing
### Wren

I'm walking back to the cabin
with Darra after supper, just the two of us.
   *I don't know how you'll take this,* she says,
   *but I want to tell you one more thing*
   *about what happened.*
      She takes a deep breath.
*Okay—here goes:*
      *My mom told me to leave your mom's*
      *purse in the car. So I did.*
I knew that—it was in the car when the police found it.
   *But I kept*
      *a little photo album*
      *I found under the front seat.*
We always wondered what happened to that!
      *I still have it.*
It's my family, not hers!
      *You can have it back.*
That album might have been little, but it was a big thing to steal.

*Yes, I want that back!* I say.
   *Why did you even want it?*

Darra flinches at my anger.
*I don't know, Wren—it was like*
*this picture-perfect family.*
*I wished Alex*
   *was my brother.*
      *That's all.*

It takes me a minute to get to: Yes.
   That is all.
   Some pictures.
   Not my actual family.
   It's okay.

Later, back at the cabin, Darra asks
   if she can see a picture
   of what my family looks like now.

   I show her one of Alex in his tracksuit,
   Mom and Dad and me behind him,
   all of us smiling
      like we are
      in every picture.

She holds it for a minute, hands it back.
   *Take good care of this,* she says.

## Gold and Purple Sky
### Darra

Our whole cabin got up early this morning to watch the sunrise. I
will never forget the gold and purple sky—just the
faintest touch of pink as the dark turned light.
The swans swam by, stretching and bending their long necks. We heard
a pair of loons call back and forth
across the water. It was magical.

Now Sam sits next to me at the arts-and-crafts table. Today is the
second-to-last day of Nature Crafts, and he's
bursting with a big surprise. He reminds
me of someone in an old-fashioned movie, ringing the doorbell
with a huge bouquet of flowers. *I made this
for you,* he says, handing me a gift.
I open it carefully, folding and saving the paper. Everyone at
the table is watching. Sam has made a box
out of curved sticks glued together in layers.
It has a lid with an acorn knob. I lift it and inside are seven
different treasures he has made or found.
A polished stone, a small piece of driftwood,
a blue feather, a perfect pinecone, a duck (I think) that he carved in
the woodwork shop. A gift certificate for

ten free breadsticks from Pizza Hut. And
his buddy tag. *I need it two more times for free swim, but at the
campfire Friday night, I'll give it to you.* I kiss
the top of his head and say, *I'll give you mine too.*
He turns bright red. It will be hard to leave on Saturday morning.
*This,* I tell him, *is the nicest present anyone has ever
given me.* He beams. *Come back next summer, Darra!*

*A Plan*
   *Wren*


Darra and I have been trying
      to come up with a plan—some way
         we could actually win
         at Drown Last. Since she
         is leaving tomorrow,
            today is our last chance.

*You take Jonna, I take Tyler . . . then . . . No, I'll take Peter, you . . .*
      but it always ends with someone
      stronger than either of us
      coming after whichever one of us
      survives until the end.

Now Darra is asking
      a different question: *Who*
         *would rescue Jeremy*
         *if he was drowning?*

We have a plan.

The whistle blows, we all dive in.
   Before Jeremy has time
   to go after anyone,
         we both dive down,
            swim behind him,
         and surface—
      me on his left side,
            Darra on his right.
            We each grab one arm,
            hold on tight,
            and don't let go.
Jeremy fights hard—twisting,
   kicking, trying
         to push us away.
      But we're determined,
      and the two of us
            are stronger than we knew.


      We keep swimming,
            until we all reach Home
            together.

## Come Back
### Darra

Tonight is my last night. All of Cabin Eight goes with me to find a
stone in the creek. Meghan is leaving too—
we each choose a stone and bring it back.
I half expect Savannah to write some kind of fashion police
remark about my clothes,
but she writes, "I'll actually miss you."
"Actually" isn't so nice, I know, but it's nothing mean about our car
or my friends or clothes, and "actually" I don't
hate Savannah either. Rachel writes,
"Thanks for teaching me to swim." I forgot that—a lot has happened in
these four weeks. Meghan: "Take Sam
home with you. (Just Kidding.)"
I take my stone out to K.C. She's sitting in the sun on the front
steps, like she has so many times before.
"Come back next summer!" she writes. I doubt I'll
be able to, but K.C. says, as she watches me read it, *There are lots of
ways we can help make that happen, Darra.*
I'd like that. I've paid so much attention to Wren—
okay, and Jeremy—I barely noticed I was making other friends. Our
cabin, and Camp Oakwood, is like—well, the way
it was to everyone else when I first got here,

that's how it is to me now. Cabin Eight is like living in a nice house
in a safe and friendly neighborhood. Now everyone
but Wren has written something on my stone.

I saved her for last. I know she's trying to think of that one
perfect thing I'll understand, that's mysterious
enough so no one else would get it.
There's nothing to forgive anymore. I know she didn't send the cop
to arrest Dad. And she didn't mean to kick me,
or pull my hair when we played Drown Last.
I remember when she was a scared little girl in the boat, petting
Archie, and I look at her now as she writes
on my stone. She hands it back to me.
"None of it was our fault," I read. I look at her. *And don't blame Bilbo
either,* she says softly, so I'm the only one to hear.
I catch my breath. She knows I blamed Bilbo?
It wasn't Bilbo's fault. It was Dad's. Later, at the campfire: *Another
session of Camp Oakwood is coming to a close,*
Mrs. Seeger says. She gives her speech. Then
Wren and Josh lead everyone in a silly song: *We wear red pajamas at
Camp Oakwood when it's hot.* I know the words
to all these songs now. When did that happen?
Sam gets an award for Most Improved Junior Boy Swimmer. The
awards ceremony goes on awhile, but I don't care.
Jeremy is sitting beside me. He's warm. I love
this. Sam's buddy tag in my pocket. Jeremy holding my hand. The door
swings open between "you know," "what happened,"
and "who knows what will happen next."

*Archie*
  *Wren*


Darra asks, *Do you want to meet*
    *my mom?*
  I answer, *Maybe.*

I'm not sure how it would feel
    to hear her voice again, or
    look her in the eye, or shake her hand.
    *I think I'll be okay with it,*
        *but let's wait till she gets here,*
        *and see how it goes.*

Now here's her car, rattling into the parking lot.
Darra is all packed. We've said goodbye.

Stacey gets out and stretches her arms
    up to the sky.
    I'm still not sure.

Darra looks at me—*Either way,*
    *it's okay with me,* she says.

Then—
　　*Archie?*
He's looking out the back window
and I'd swear
he knows me.


I walk with Darra over to the car.
She opens the back door, takes Archie out,
　　holds him in her arms and turns to me.
　　*Archie,* she whispers,
　　*you remember Wren.*


She hands her cat to me.
　　He licks my face,
　　purrs in my ear.


　　I nod.


*Mom,* says Darra.
Stacey Monson looks at us.


　　*This is my friend,*
　　*Wren Abbott.*

*Diving Deeper: Notes on Form*

Wren's poems are written in free verse—the placement of words on the page is something like musical notation. In Part One, the numbered sections are one way of indicating the passage of time.

Darra's poems are written in a form invented for this book. The last words of the long lines, when read down the right side of the page, give further insight into her story.

Like Wren, you may wonder how Darra could love her father when he treated her and her mother so badly. In Part Two, the words at the ends of the long lines are Darra's memories of her father from the time before Wren's story begins.

When Wren and Darra meet at Camp Oakwood, you know what happened when they were eight, but you have heard it all from Wren's point of view. How did Darra experience the same event? In Part Three, the end-word sentences tell what she remembers from the other side of the door.

These sentences are not punctuated, since the punctuation of the poem goes with the other part of the story. If there is more than one sentence in the end-words of a single poem, there is a stanza break between those sentences. (There are also a few stanza breaks that do not indicate a new sentence in the end-word story.)

## Acknowledgments

*Hidden* is not based on any real events or people. The story begins in a fictional city in central Michigan. Camp Oakwood, also fictional, is located in Michigan's beautiful Upper Peninsula.

I thank:

The Indiana Arts Commission and the National Endowment for the Arts for their generous fellowships.

Frances Foster for wise and careful editing.

Lisa Graff and Susan Dobinick and everyone at Farrar Straus Giroux.

Friends and fellow writers: Christianne Balk, Martha Christina, Ann Colbert, Clydia Early, Claire Ewart, Laurie Gray, Paula Kent, Gretchen Liuzzi, Joe and Mary Macneil, Ketu Oladuwa, Yvonne Ramsey, Suzanne Scollon, Lisa Tsetse, Ingrid Wendt, and the Society for Children's Book Writers and Illustrators, especially the Fort Wayne, Indiana writers group.

My large extended family for answers to questions such as "Would an eight-year-old fit through a pet door?" Special thanks to my brother Richard (Frosty) and his children, Jackson and Dana.

My son Lloyd and his wife, Penny, and their children, Cameron Ian and Jordan Tate; my son Glen; and my husband, Chad, for ideas, encouragement, and love.

# WRITE A POEM WITH A HIDDEN MESSAGE

Write a sentence of five to ten words describing something you have seen or heard yesterday or today.

Write the words of your sentence down the right side of the page.

Then write a poem that includes the words you have written but is about something different. The poem and the sentence might accidentally turn out to be related, but don't try to connect them on purpose.

*Here's a worksheet that might help. Use as many hidden words as you can.*

Sentence: _____

_____.

Hidden Words *(your sentence, written down the page)*:

                                               _____

                                               _____

                                               _____

                                               _____

                                               _____

                                               _____

                                               _____

                                               _____

                                               _____

# A CONVERSATION WITH
# HELEN FROST

**What sparked your imagination for *Hidden*?**

*Hidden* began as a very different story, and as I was trying to understand why Wren was who she was, I realized that something serious
had happened to her when she was younger. I imagined what that might
have been, and the first part of the story was born.

**Did any current events or news stories inspire *Hidden* in any way?**

I didn't read about anything like this before I wrote the story, but the
week that *Hidden* was published, there were three instances in my
community of cars stolen with children inside them, unbeknownst to
the car thieves. All of the children were returned safely to their homes,
and an article in our local newspaper warned parents about the danger
of leaving children unattended in cars.

**Did you ever go to summer camp?**

I went to one overnight camp when I was twelve, and later I worked as
a camp counselor at several different camps. I love all the traditions of
summer camps and the close friendships that are formed there. I'm still
friends with some of the people I first met at summer camp. And
"Drown Last" was a game I learned in a Junior Lifesaving class.

**How did you decide on the poetic structures for *Hidden*?**

In my notebooks, where I first started writing Wren's part of the story, I was writing in prose. But the story was so intense, it needed something to allow the reader time to take it in. I reached for my "poetry toolbox" and decided that line breaks, with movement across the page, would give the story some breathing room, so I wrote that part of the story in free verse.

In part two of the book, Darra's story is furthered by the last words on the right side of the page.

**What is it like to write a story within a story?**

I enjoy it! Language has so many deep connections, and using a word in two ways at once brings those connections into focus, giving a story more depth and texture.

**Why did you decide to give each voice a different poetic structure?**

I think about what each voice requires and look for a way to enhance that.

**What was the biggest challenge you faced while writing *Hidden*?**

As I mentioned, it began as a very different story. It was a challenge to separate the two stories and figure out which one I most wanted to tell.

**Do you have a favorite poetic structure that you've invented for a book?**

*The Braid* was amazing because it was so demanding, and it worked for the entire book! I also enjoyed the structure of *Diamond Willow* because I had a diamond willow stick suspended from the ceiling in my writing room, and I looked at it as I wrote; the diamonds in the stick became the shapes of the poems.

**What made you decide to write your books in different poetic forms?**

I began, in *Keesha's House* and *Room 214*, by using traditional forms already invented. Then I got interested in inventing my own book-length forms, and I love all the possibilities that have opened up.

**Who are your favorite poets?**

I have too many favorites to name—poets who represent different centuries, different countries, different styles of writing. Some write for adults, some write for children, some write for all ages. I like to tell people to remember "811" in your library, the same way you remember 911 as an emergency telephone number. I believe that poetry can save lives, and 811 is the Dewey Decimal call number of the section in the library where you will find it.

**What sparked your interest in poetry?**

My mother knew many poems by heart and often recited them as we walked or whenever a poem came to her. I first loved the music of poetry, and then I came to love the images and meaning. My father was a storyteller—he could invent stories that would keep us interested for a long time. And now I'm combining poetry and story in my novels-in-poems.

Jack knows things his teachers could never teach. Natalie knows you don't just *lose* a person, especially not a father. Sharrell saves her friend's life. All these secrets come together like poetry among the students of Room 214.

Read on for a sneak peek of

*Room 214: A Year in Poems*

# Great Explorers, Room 214

MRS. WILLIAMS

I tape the children's pictures of the great explorers—Leif
Eriksson, Magellan, Sacagawea and York and Lewis and Clark—
on the wall around our big 3-D relief

map. Across the room, taped on windows, leaves from the park,
pressed between waxed paper, catch the light
the morning sun shines in. My work

starts early. It's never really done. Last night
the moon kept me awake and I
thought about these kids—what might

be on their minds? What makes them happy? Sad? Why
does Maria tear her papers into shreds?
What puts that twinkle in Jaquanna's eye?

I sometimes get the feeling that Eddie dreads
each school day. I wonder what's going on with Sam—
yesterday when they all put their heads

down, he fell asleep in seconds flat. Why did Andrew slam
his math book shut, the other day when I came in?
Does Rosa have warm clothes? Does Dustin understand

the work we're doing? And then there's Ben,
so happy whenever his team's
winning, so miserable when

they lose. I write my plans: Reading—themes
of love and courage. Social studies—the explorers' dreams.

Sunlight, orange leaves,
their veins like veins in my hands—
leaves, light, hands, dancing.

*NAOMI*

# Grandma Keeps Forgetting

### VONDA

Grandma keeps forgetting that my grandpa died.
She asks us where he is, why he's been gone
so long. And if we say, *Remember?*

*He had a heart attack,* she tries to remember
but she can't. We have to tell her that he died.
That makes her mad. So now we say he's gone

to someplace nice. She's glad he hasn't gone
to war again. It wasn't always like this. I remember
once when I was little, we found a bird that died.

*What's "died"?* I asked, and Grandma said, *The bird is gone,
    but we remember.*

# Late Again
## SAM

We got evicted yesterday. I came home and all my
stuff was in a box outside the door.
Me, my mom, my sister, and her baby, Ty,
had to sleep in my mom's brother's car.
I'm late again. I hope nobody asks me why.

It's hard to sleep with so much traffic going by.
There's no alarm clock in my uncle's car.
My clothes are dirty. I couldn't comb my hair. I
know the kids are thinking, *You're
late again.* At least nobody's asking why.

Should I make up a story? They'll guess it's a lie,
and anything I'd say, they've heard before.
It's hard to get my work done, but I'll try.
Sometimes Mrs. Williams lets me sleep. So far
she hasn't said, *You're late again. Why?*

# Without My Bike
*JON*

My bike is blue. Black stripes. And now it's gone.
I want to know who took it. Why? And where?

My bike is part of me. We're like the wind
together, going anywhere we want.

Without my bike, my legs are empty. It
has tricks you have to know to ride it right,

like: jerk the handlebars before you jump,
and push them down again to get more speed.

It's like my bike and me are brothers. Friends
that never fight. A new one wouldn't be

the same. I want my own bike back. It's blue.
Black stripes. It whistles when you go real fast.

# Make a Few Adjustments

## ANDREW

Jon just left his bike lying in the street
like he don't care. Anybody could've stole it.
I ain't no thief, but I'm the one that took
it home. I gotta fix that squeaky noise it makes.
Can't stand it! You get yourself a bike,
you should take care of it. I wonder

if Jon knows how the derailleur works. Wonder
if he ever greases it. He rides down the street
like he thinks he got some kinda magic bike,
then he leaves it lying outside in the rain! I know he's
        missing it—
I'll put it back tomorrow, after I make
a few adjustments. Let him think somebody took

it, for real—maybe he'll start taking
better care of it. Lately I been wondering
if you can make
a living fixing bikes. There's a dude on my street
that can drive a car one block and tell you what it
needs to make it run right. I can do that with bikes,

but not so many people need their bikes
fixed. So, I don't know—Dad says, *Keep taking*

*math.* He knows I'm good at it,
but my teachers never see that. I wonder
what Mrs. Williams meant: *Andrew, you're a one-way street—*
that thing she said when she was trying to make

me tell her why I slammed my book shut. (Not *make*
me, exactly. She just asked.) The day I rode Jon's bike
home, I found $20 in the street.
I put it in my math book, just taking
care of it, that's all. But I been wondering
what she meant by *one-way street.* Maybe it

means I don't tell her what I'm thinking. It
gets to be a habit. Last year, my teacher made
me mad—so suspicious all the time. Wonder
why he didn't like me. His voice sounded like Jon's bike—
faster he talked, higher it got. But I take
Mrs. Williams's point. I could maybe open up my "street"

a little. Tell her I want to take that test for Gifted—wonder
if I'm smart enough. Some ways, yes—like, I can make bikes
out of parts. Got one now, ready for its test run on the street.

Black/orange flower
flying, lands on a dark branch—
monarch butterfly.

*NAOMI*

# Suki

### RYAN

Suki's gone. Our cat.
I looked in the hall closet.
The cellar. Nowhere.

We've had her almost three years.
She wouldn't just leave. Would she?

∞

Three days. I won't cry.
Her bed empty by the door.
All our rooms quiet.

Who would think one missing cat
could make a whole house silent?

# Pepperoni Was My Dog

### RICHARD

I know how Ryan feels. Suki, his white cat—she's

Missing. He wants me to help him look, but
I don't know his cat. I don't know where
Suki sleeps or what she eats. In other words,
Suki isn't Pepperoni.

Pepperoni was my dog. He died. Now
Every day when I come home from school,
Pepperoni doesn't thump his tail.
Pepperoni doesn't curl beside me on the couch,
Even if I whistle and pat the place he likes.
Rawhide bones and chewed up toys aren't left all
Over the back yard. My ears are empty from the
Noises Pepperoni doesn't make.
I know how much space one cat or dog can fill.

# Suki

*RYAN*

She came home! She ate
and left again. I followed.
She's under the porch.

You can hear something in there.
Suki lies down, curls up—purrrrrrr

∞

Four kittens! Two white
like Suki. One gray and brown.
One black as midnight.

You have to lift a loose board
to see them. Careful, don't touch!

∞

*Midnight.* Small white star
above his right eye. Suki
lets me pick him up.

I hold his fur to my cheek.
His heart beats against my skin.

# One Small Kitten
### MANUEL

*Now what do we want with a cat?*
That's all my mama got to say.
She won't listen. I tell her that
it's just a kitten, brown and gray.

Ryan says I can have it when
it's big enough to give away.
Mama says *No!* I say again,
Just a small kitten, brown and gray.

I know a good place to keep it—
a box in the downstairs hallway.
I measured, and the box will fit
my soft-eyed kitten, brown and gray.

*You got four sisters! There's enough*
*mouths to feed! Now who's going to pay*
*for cat food?* But—it won't eat much.
Just one kitten. It's brown and gray

and it likes me. It licks my hand
with its sandpaper tongue. Someday
I'll have a big house, just me and
my own kitten. Soft, brown, and gray.

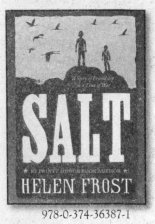

# BLOOD PRICE

## TANYA HUFF

**D A W  B O O K S ,  I N C .**
**DONALD  A.  WOLLHEIM,  FOUNDER**
375 Hudson Street, New York, NY 10014

**ELIZABETH R. WOLLHEIM**
**SHEILA E. GILBERT**
**PUBLISHERS**

FOR JOHN, who, from the beginning, has been more than understanding about phone calls, photocopying, trips to the post office, arriving late, leaving early, and occasionally not showing up at all. Thanks.

# One

Ian shoved his hands deep in his pockets and scowled down the length of the empty subway platform. His hands were freezing, he was in a bitch of a bad mood, and he had no idea why he'd agreed to meet Coreen at her apartment. All things considered, neutral ground might have been a better idea. He shifted his scowl to the LED clock hanging from the ceiling. 12:17. Thirteen minutes to get from Eglinton West to Wilson Station, six blocks worth of bus ride, and then a three block run to Coreen's. It couldn't be done.

*I'm going to be late. She's going to be pissed. And there goes our chance to make up.* He sighed. It had taken two hours of arguing on the phone to get her to agree to a meeting. Maintaining a relationship with Coreen might be time-consuming, but it sure as hell wasn't boring. Lord, but the woman had a temper. . . . His lips curled up into a smile almost without him willing the motion; the flip side of that temper made all the effort of staying on the roller coaster worthwhile. The smile broadened. Coreen packed a lot of punch for a woman barely five foot two.

He glanced up at the clock again.

*Where the hell was the train?*

12:20.

*Be there by 12:30 or forget it*, she'd said, completely ignoring the fact that on Sunday the Toronto Transit Commission, the ubiquitous TTC, drastically cut back on the number of trains and at this hour he'd be lucky to get the last one they ran.

Looking at the bright side, when he finally got there, given the time of night and the fact that they both had an eight o'clock class, he'd have to stay over. He sighed. *If she'll even let me into her apartment.*

He wandered down to the southernmost end of the platform and peered into the tunnel. No sign of lights, but he could feel wind against his face and that usually meant the train wasn't far. He coughed as he turned away. It smelled like something had died down there; smelled like it did at the cottage when a mouse got between the walls and rotted.

"Big mother of a mouse," he muttered, rubbing his fist against his nose. The stench caught in his lungs and he coughed again. It was funny the tricks the mind played; now that he was aware of it, the smell seemed to be getting stronger.

And then he heard what could only be footsteps coming up the tunnel, out of the darkness. Heavy footsteps, not at all like a worker hurrying to beat the train after a day's overtime, nor like a bum staggering for the safety of the platform. Heavy footsteps, purposefully advancing toward his back.

Ian gloried in the sharp terror that started his heart thudding in his chest and trapped his breath in his throat. He knew very well that when he turned, when he looked, the explanation would be prosaic, so he froze and enjoyed the unknown while it remained unknown, delighted in the adrenaline rush of fear that made every sense more alive and made the seconds stretch to hours.

He didn't turn until the footsteps moved up the half dozen cement stairs and onto the platform.

Then it was too late.

He almost didn't have time to scream.

\* \* \*

Tucking her chin down into her coat—it might be April but it was still damp and cold, with no sign of spring— Vicki Nelson stepped off the Eglinton bus and into the subway station.

"Well, that was a disaster," she muttered. The elderly gentleman who had exited the bus right behind her made an inquiring noise. She turned a bland stare in his general direction, then picked up her pace. *So I'm not only "lousy company, and so uptight I squeak," but I also talk to myself.* She sighed. Lawrence was pretty, but he wasn't her type. She hadn't met a man who was her type since she'd left the police force eight months before. *I should've known this was going to happen when I agreed to go out with a man significantly better looking than I am. I don't know why I accepted the invitation.*

That wasn't exactly true; she'd accepted the invitation because she was lonely. She knew it, she just had no intention of admitting it.

She was halfway down the first set of stairs leading to the southbound platform when she heard the scream. Or rather the half-scream. It choked off in mid-wail. One leap took her to the first landing. From where she stood, she could see only half of each platform through the glass and no indication of which side the trouble was on. The south was closer, faster.

Bounding down two, and then three steps at a time she yelled, "Call the police!" Even if no one heard her, it might scare off the cause of the scream.

Nine years on the force and she'd never used her gun. She wanted it now. In nine years on the force she'd never heard a scream like that.

*"What the hell do you think you're doing?"* the more rational part of her brain shrieked. *"You don't have a weapon! You don't have backup! You don't have any idea of what's going on down there! Eight months off the force and you've forgotten everything they ever taught you! What the hell are you trying to prove?"*

Vicki ignored the voice and kept moving. Maybe she was trying to prove something. So what.

When she exploded out onto the platform, she immediately realized she'd chosen the wrong side and for just an instant, she was glad of it.

A great spray of blood arced up the orange tiles of the station wall, feathering out from a thick red stream to a delicate pattern of crimson drops. On the floor below, his eyes and mouth open above the mangled ruin of his throat, lay a young man. No: the body of a young man.

The dinner she'd so recently eaten rose to the back of

Vicki's throat, but walls built during the investigations of other deaths slammed into place and she forced it down.

The wind in the tunnel began to pick up and she could hear the northbound train approaching. It sounded close.

*Sweet Jesus, that's all we need.* At 12:35 on a Sunday night it was entirely possible that the train would be nearly empty, no one would get off, and no one would notice the corpse and the blood-spattered wall down at the southernmost end of the northbound platform. Given the way of the world, however, it was more likely that a group of children and a little old lady with a weak heart would pile out of the last carriage and come face-to-face with the staring eyes and mutely screaming mouth of a fresh corpse.

Only one solution presented itself.

The roar of the train filled the station as, heart pounding and adrenaline singing in her ears, Vicki leapt down onto the southbound tracks. The wooden step over the live rail was too far away, almost centered in the line of concrete pillars, so she jumped, trying not to think of the however many million volts of electricity the thing carried turning her to charcoal. She tottered for a moment on the edge of the divider, cursing her full-length coat and wishing she'd worn a jacket, and then, although she knew it was the stupidist thing she could do, she looked toward the oncoming train.

*How did it get so close?* The light was blinding, the roar deafening. She froze, caught in the glare, sure that if she continued she'd fall and the metal wheels of the beast would cut her to shreds.

Then something man-height flickered across the northbound tunnel. She didn't see much, just a billowing shadow, black against the growing headlight, but it jerked her out of immobility and down onto the track.

Cinders crunched under her boots, metal rang, then she had her hands on the edge of the platform and was flinging herself into the air. The world filled with sound and light and something brushed lightly against her sole.

Her hands were sticky, covered with blood, but it wasn't hers and at the moment that was all that mattered.

Before the train stopped, she'd flung her coat over the body and grabbed her ID.

The center-man stuck his head out.

Vicki flipped the leather folder in his direction and barked, "Close the doors! Now!"

The doors, not quite open, closed.

She remembered to breathe again and when the center-man's head reappeared, snapped, "Have the driver get the police on the radio. Tell them it's a 10-33 . . . never mind what that means!" She saw the question coming. "They'll know! And don't forget to tell them where it is." People had done stupider things in emergencies. As he ducked back into the train, she looked down at her card case and sighed, then lifted one gory finger to push her glasses back up her nose. A private investigator's ID meant absolutely nothing in a case like this, but people responded to the appearance of authority, not the particulars.

She moved a little farther from the body. Up close, the smell of blood and urine—the front of the boy's jeans was soaked—easily overcame the metallic odors of the subway. A lone face peered out through the window of the closest car. She snarled at it and settled down to wait.

Less than three minutes later, Vicki heard the faint sound of sirens up on the street. She almost cheered. It had been the longest three minutes of her life.

She'd spent them thinking, adding together the spray of blood and the position of the body and not liking the total.

Nothing that she knew of could strike a single blow strong enough to tear through flesh like tissue paper and fast enough that the victim had no time to struggle. Nothing. But something had.

And it was down in the tunnels.

She twisted until she could see into the darkness beyond the end of the train. The hair on the back of her neck rose. What did the shadows hide, she wondered. Her skin crawled, not entirely because of the cold. She'd never considered herself an overly imaginative woman and she knew the killer had to be long gone, but *something* lingered in that tunnel.

The distinctive slam of police boots against tile brought

her around, hands held carefully out from her sides. Police called to a violent murder, finding someone covered in blood standing over the body, could be excused if they jumped to a conclusion or two.

The situation got chaotic for a few minutes, but fortunately four of the six constables had heard of "Victory" Nelson and after apologies had been exchanged all around, they got to work.

". . . my coat over the body, had the driver call the police, and waited." Vicki watched Police Constable West scribbling madly in his occurrence book and hid a grin. She could remember being that young and that intense. Barely. When he looked up, she nodded at the body and asked, "Do you want to see?"

"Uh, no!" After a second he added, a little sheepishly, "That is, we shouldn't disturb anything before homicide gets here."

Homicide. Vicki's stomach lurched and her mood nosedived. She'd forgotten she wasn't in charge. Forgotten she was nothing more than a witness—first on the scene and that only because she'd done some pretty stupid things to get there. The uniforms had made it seem like old times but homicide . . . her department. No, not hers any longer. She pushed her glasses up her nose with the back of her wrist.

PC West, caught staring, dropped his gaze in confusion. "Uh, I don't think anyone would mind if you cleaned the blood off your hands."

"Thanks." Vicki managed a smile but ignored the unasked question. How well she could see, or how little she could see, was nobody's business but hers. Let another round of rumors start making its way through the force. "If you wouldn't mind grabbing a couple of tissues out of my bag. . . ."

The young constable dipped a tentative hand into the huge black leather purse and actually looked relieved when he removed it holding the tissue and still in possession of all his fingers. Vicki's bag had been legendary throughout Metro and the boroughs.

Most of the blood on her hands had dried to reddish brown flakes and the little that hadn't the tissue merely smeared around. She scrubbed at it anyway, feeling rather like Lady MacBeth.

"Destroying the evidence?"

*Celluci,* she thought. *They had to send Celluci. That bastard always walked too quietly.* She and Mike Celluci had not parted on the best of terms but, by the time she turned to face him, she managed to school her expression.

"Just trying to make life more difficult for you." The voice and the smile that went with it were patently false.

He nodded, an overly long curl of dark brown hair falling into his face. "Always the best idea to play to your strengths." Then his eyes went past her to the body. "Give your statement to Dave." Behind him, his partner waved two fingers. "I'll talk to you later. This your coat?"

"Yeah, it's mine." Vicki watched him lift the edge of the blood-soaked fabric and knew that for the moment nothing existed for him but the body and its immediate surroundings. Although their methods differed, he was as intense in the performance of his duties as she was— *had been,* she corrected herself silently—and the undeclared competition between them had added an edge to many an investigation. Including a number neither of them were on.

"Vicki?"

She unclenched her jaw and, still scrubbing at her hands, followed Dave Graham a few meters up the platform.

Dave, who had been partnered with Mike Celluci for only a month when Vicki left the force and the final screaming match had occurred, smiled a little self-consciously and said, "How about we just do this by the book?"

Vicki released a breath she didn't know she'd been holding. "Sure, that'd be fine." Taking refuge from emotions in police procedure—a worldwide law enforcement tradition.

While they talked, the subway train, now empty of passengers, pulled slowly out of the station.

". . . responding to the scream you ran down onto the southbound platform, then crossed the tracks in front of a northbound train to reach the body. While crossing the tracks . . ."

Inwardly, Vicki cringed. Dave Graham was one of the least judgmental men in existence, but even he couldn't keep his opinion of that stunt from showing in his voice.

". . . you saw a man-shaped form in what appeared to be a loose, flowing garment cross between you and the lights. Is that it?"

"Essentially." Stripped of all the carefully recorded details, it sounded like such a stupid thing to have done.

"Right." He closed the notebook and scratched at the side of his nose. "You, uh, going to stick around?"

Vicki squinted as the police photographer snapped off another quick series of shots. She couldn't see Mike, but she could hear him down in the tunnel barking commands in his best "God's gift to the Criminal Investigations Bureau" voice. Down in the tunnel . . . The hair on the back of her neck rose again as she remembered the feeling of *something* lingering, something dark and, well if she had to put a name to it, evil. She suddenly wanted to warn Celluci to be careful. She didn't. She knew how he'd react. How *she'd* react if their positions were reversed.

"Vicki? You sticking around?"

It was on the tip of her tongue to say no, that they knew where to find her if they needed further information, but curiosity—about what the police would find, about how long she could remain so close to the job she'd loved and not fall apart—turned the no into a grudging, "For a while." She'd be damned if she'd run away.

As she watched, Celluci came up the stairs onto the platform and spoke to the ident man, sweeping one arm back along the tracks. The ident man protested that he needed a certain amount of light to do his job, but Celluci cut him off. With a disgusted snort, he picked up his case and headed for the tunnel.

*Charming as ever,* Vicki thought as Celluci scooped her coat off the floor and made his way toward her, detouring slightly around the coroner's men who were finally zipping the body into its orange plastic bag. "Don't tell me," she called as soon as he was close enough, her voice carefully dry, almost sarcastic, and hopefully showing no indication of the churning emotions that had her gut tied in knots. "The only prints on the scene are mine?'' There were, of course, a multitude of prints on the scene, none of which had been identified—that was for downtown—but the bloody handprints Vicki had scattered around were obvious.

"Dead on, Sherlock." He tossed her the coat. "And the blood trail leads into a workman's alcove and stops."

Vicki frowned as she reconstructed what had to have happened just before she reached the platform. "You checked the southbound side?"

"That's where we lost the trail." His tone added, *Don't teach Grandpa to suck eggs.* He held up a hand to forestall the next question. "I had one of the uniforms talk to the old man while Dave was dealing with you, but he's hysterical. He keeps going on about Armageddon. His son-in-law's coming to pick him up and I'll go see him tomorrow."

Vicki shot a glance across the station where the old man who had followed her off the bus and down the stairs sat talking to a policewoman. Even at a distance he didn't look good. His face was gray and he appeared to be babbling uncontrollably, one scrawny, swollen-knuckled hand clutching at the constable's sleeve. Turning her attention back to her companion, she asked, "What about the subway? You closed it for the night?"

"Yeah." Mike waved toward the end of the platform. "I want Jake to dust that alcove." Intermittent flashes of light indicated the photographer was still at work. "It's not the sort of case where we can get in and out in a couple of minutes." He shoved his hands into his overcoat pockets and scowled. "Although the way the transit commission squawked you'd think we were shutting it down in rush hour to pick up someone for littering."

"What, uh, sort of case is it?" Vicki asked—as close as she could get to asking if he, too, felt it, whatever *it* turned out to be.

He shrugged. "You tell me; you seem to have gone to a great deal of trouble to land right in the middle of this."

"I was here," she snapped. "Would you have preferred that I ignore it?"

"You had no weapon, no backup, no idea of what was

going down.'' Celucci ticked off an identical litany to the one she'd read herself earlier. "You can't have forgotten everything in eight months.''

"And what would you have done?'' she spat through clenched teeth.

"I wouldn't have tried to kill myself just to prove I still could.''

The silence that fell landed like a load of cement blocks and Vicki gritted her teeth under its weight. Was that what she'd been doing? She looked down at the toes of her boots, then up at Mike. At five ten she didn't look up to many men but Celluci, at six four, practically made her feel petite. She hated feeling petite. "If we're going to rehash my leaving the force again, I'm out of here.''

He held up both hands in a gesture of weary surrender. "You're right. As usual. I'm sorry. We're not going to rehash anything.''

"You brought it up.'' She sounded hostile; she didn't care. She should've followed her instincts and left the moment she'd given her statement. She had to have been out of her mind, putting herself in this position, staying in Celluci's reach.

A muscle in his jaw jumped. "I said I was sorry. Go ahead, be superwoman if you want to, but maybe,'' he added, his voice tight, "I don't want to see you get killed. *Maybe*, I'm not willing to toss aside eight years of friendship. . . .''

"Friendship?'' Vicki felt her eyebrows rise.

Celluci drove his hands into his hair, yanking them through the curls, a gesture he used when he was trying very hard to keep his temper. "Maybe I'm not willing to toss aside four years of friendship and four years of sex because of a stupid disagreement!''

"Just sex? That's it?'' Vicki took the easy way out, ignoring the more loaded topic of their *disagreement*. A shortage of things to fight about had never been one of their problems. "Well, it wasn't just sex to me, Detective!''

They were both yelling now.

"Did I say it was just sex?'' He spread his arms wide, his voice booming off the tiled walls of the subway